mary-kate olsen   **ashley** olsen

so little time

Check out these other great
so little time
titles:

mary-kate olsen   **ashley** olsen

so little time

secret crush

By Jacqueline Carrol

Based on the teleplay by Michael Baser and Frank Dungan

HarperEntertainment
An Imprint of HarperCollins*Publishers*

A PARACHUTE PRESS BOOK

A PARACHUTE PRESS BOOK

Parachute Publishing, L.L.C.
156 Fifth Avenue, Suite 302
New York, NY 10010

Published by

▰ HarperEntertainment

An *Imprint of* HarperCollins*Publishers*
10 East 53rd Street, New York, NY 10022-5299

ISBN 0-06-008808-7

HarperCollins®, ▰®, and HarperEntertainment™ are trademarks of HarperCollins Publishers Inc.

First printing: November 2002

Printed in the United States of America

Visit HarperEntertainment on the World Wide Web at
www.harpercollins.com

10 9 8 7 6 5 4 3 2 1

chapter
one

"**H**i, everybody!" fourteen-year-old Chloe Carlson said in a bright, energetic voice as she walked into the kitchen Friday afternoon. "Isn't this a gorgeous day?"

"It certainly is," Manuelo, the Carlsons' cook and housekeeper, agreed. He eyed Chloe. "What happened in school today?" he asked. "You're perky, but never *this* perky."

"I bet she met a cute boy," Tedi said. She was a fashion model who worked with Chloe's mom, Macy.

"For your information, I'm practicing my 'happy voice,'" Chloe replied. "I want to make sure I'm totally cheerful and friendly when I go to the retirement home." She pushed her long, wavy blond hair away from her face and gestured at her plain blouse and skirt. "And I decided to kind of dress down. No flashy clothes or anything."

"The retirement home?" Macy repeated. She whipped

out her Palm Pilot. "Let's see…today is Friday, right?"

Chloe grinned. Her mother was a busy, successful fashion designer. She and Chloe's dad, Jake, used to work together. But a few months ago they decided to separate—both personally and professionally. Now Macy ran the business by herself and needed her Palm to keep track of everything that went on.

"Got it," Macy announced. "Community service, right? Your dad is picking you up in…" She glanced at her watch. "Seven minutes." Macy and Jake were still really good friends, but Jake now lived in a trailer on Malibu Beach. Chloe and her twin sister, Riley, lived in the beach house with their mom.

"Right!" Chloe said enthusiastically. "He's taking me to the Sunnyview Retirement Home! Isn't that awesome?"

"Really?" Tedi crossed her mile-long legs. "Not that community service isn't cool, but I thought for sure you had a date. I mean, you're practically chirping."

"Sorry to disappoint you, Tedi—no date today," Chloe said. "Community service is way more important."

[Chloe: Community service IS way more important than dating. But to tell you the truth, I'm not that excited about going to Sunnyview. I mean, I'm not even sure what I'm supposed to do. Hang out with old people? Play checkers and bingo? It doesn't sound like much fun to me. Oh, well…

that's what I get for signing up for a project at the last minute. At least I'm getting extra credit at school. I just hope my "happy voice" holds up.]

"Riley signed up for something, too, didn't she?" Macy asked, sipping some coffee.

"Yup, and I'm ready to go." Riley bounded into the room. She was wearing denim overalls and heavy work boots. A pair of thick gloves poked from one of her pockets, and she'd tied her blond hair back with a red bandanna. "How do I look?"

"Like part of a road crew," Manuelo said.

"Or you could stick a piece of hay in your mouth and you'd fit right in on a farm," Tedi suggested.

Riley laughed. "Actually, you're almost right, Tedi."

"You'll be plowing fields?" Tedi asked.

"No, but remember the awful library fire?" Riley asked. "Well, they're almost finished rebuilding the library, but the garden in back still needs a lot of work."

"Ah, that's where your community service comes in," Manuelo said. "You're going to help restore it."

Riley nodded. "We have to get it done in time for the big reopening of the library—and that's in a week!"

Chloe sighed and plopped down at the table. "I would have liked to work at the garden," she said. "It sounds like fun."

Pepper, their black-and-white cocker spaniel, dropped her chew-toy and sat at Chloe's feet, hoping there might be food.

Manuelo raised his eyebrows in surprise. "Chloe and gardening—now there's a strange combination. Why, I remember a certain avocado pit that died a lonely, thirsty death before it even had a chance to sprout."

"That was in first grade!" Chloe protested. But Manuelo was right. He'd worked for the Carlsons for years and was practically part of the family. He knew she wasn't into plants. "Anyway, this isn't about gardening."

"It's not?" Tedi asked.

Chloe shook her head. "It's about guys."

"I thought it was about community service," Macy said.

"Well, sure, but if a bunch of cool guys happen to be around, that makes it even better," Chloe explained. "And some of the coolest ones are working at the library—Dean Spencer and Shane Howell."

"Don't worry, Chloe." Riley smiled wide. "I'll make sure I set aside time to give you a full report on their hotness."

"Thanks a lot," Chloe said.

The kitchen door opened and their next-door neighbor, Larry Slotnick, walked in—without knocking, as usual. Like Riley and Chloe, Larry was a freshman at West Malibu High. He was tall and lanky, with a goofy, big-mouthed grin and spiky brown hair.

Today, like Riley, he wore overalls and work boots. Unlike Riley, he wore a bright yellow hard hat.

"Hi, Larry. Love the hat," Tedi said.

"Thanks!" Larry held up a plastic shopping bag. "I got one for you, too, Riley." His brown eyes lit up as he smiled at her.

"Larry, I don't think we need hard hats," Riley declared. "We're working in a garden, not a construction site."

"Are you working at the library, too, Larry?" Macy asked.

Larry nodded happily. "With Riley. Isn't that great?"

[<u>Chloe</u>: In case you haven't noticed, Larry has a major crush on my sister. He's had it forever. She likes him, too, but not—repeat NOT—that way. Besides, she already has a boyfriend, Alex Zimmer.]

"We can talk hats later, Larry. Let's go," Riley said. She headed for the door.

As Larry followed, he tripped over Pepper's chew-toy. "Whoa!" He stumbled into a counter and banged his head against a cabinet door. He grinned and rapped his knuckles on his hard hat. "Good thing I wore this, huh? It came in handy already!"

Riley rolled her eyes.

Chloe giggled. Okay, so not every guy working at the garden was cool.

Riley opened the door and looked out. "Chloe, Dad just drove up."

"Great!" Chloe said, putting the chirp back into her

voice. She stood up and smoothed her long skirt. Sunnyview would probably be boring, but still, she was going to give it her best shot.

Smiling brightly, Chloe followed her sister and Larry out the door.

"Wow," Riley said. She stood in the back garden of the library with the other volunteers, gazing at the trampled bushes, sooty soil, and toppled sculptures. George Watkins, one of the supervisors of the library restoration, stood with them. "This is…this is—"

"A wreck," Lauren Shears declared. She was a sophomore with dark hair and lots of black eye makeup.

Shane Howell nodded. "A disaster," he agreed. A junior, he had light brown eyes and wore his sandy hair in a brush cut.

"Catastrophe," Larry declared.

"Total devastation," Dean Spencer said. Dean was a junior, too, a tall, blond star of the basketball team.

Riley kept staring around. She'd walked by here a few times after the fire, but this was the first time she'd seen it up close.

"It's a mess, that's for sure," Mr. Watkins agreed. "The bad news is, it has to be ready for the grand opening next Saturday."

Dean shook his head doubtfully. "That gives us only a week."

"Yeah, it's going to be tough," Shane agreed.

"What's the good news?" Larry asked.

Mr. Watkins chuckled. "The good news is I've got you guys. And I know I can count on you, right?"

Of course, Riley thought. After all, we volunteered. "Don't worry, we can do it," she declared.

"That's the spirit!" George said. "Now, I'm heading up the restoration inside the library. I'll be able to help a little out here, but it's mostly your show. So you need to come up with a game plan."

Riley glanced around the garden again. "I guess the first thing to do is get everything out of the way, like the sculptures and the benches," she said. She pointed to a grassy area that hadn't been ruined. "We could put them over there and work on them later. Then—"

"Whoa, wait, Riley," George interrupted. "That sounds good, but you guys should get organized first. Pick someone to be in charge."

Riley looked at the other kids. Nobody seemed to want to volunteer. "I'll do it," she said.

George looked doubtful. "No offense, but you're only a freshman, right?"

"Yes, but I can handle it," Riley assured him.

"I don't know. I was thinking someone older might be better." George glanced at the three older kids.

"Not me," Shane said. "I'm ready to work, but I don't want to be the boss."

"Me neither," Lauren said. "I don't know enough about gardening."

Dean shook his head. "I've got tons of other stuff to do besides this. I don't really have time to be in charge."

"Nobody would be better than Riley, Mr. Watkins," Larry declared. "She's totally responsible."

"Thanks, Larry," Riley said. Larry could be a pain sometimes, but he was definitely loyal. "Really, Mr. Watkins, just because I'm younger doesn't mean I can't do it," she argued. "Just give me a chance and I'll prove it." She paused. "And besides, nobody else wants the job."

"You do have a point there," George said. "Okay, Riley. You're in."

"Thanks, Mr. Watkins," Riley said. "I'll do a great job, I promise. We all will."

"Just remember, if things get out of hand, come to me right away," he said.

"Definitely," Riley agreed.

"I brought some rakes and hoes," George said, pointing to a bunch of tools near one of the shade trees. "And some sawhorses—you'll probably need to cut more slats for the benches. I didn't get a power saw, though, so—"

"It's okay, Mr. Watkins, we'll get one," Riley declared. "Just leave everything to us."

George took a last look at the garden. "Okay, I'll let you get to it. Remember, I'm counting on you." He patted Riley on the shoulder and strode away.

Riley took a deep breath. The garden was in her hands now, and she was psyched. "Okay, let's get started," she told the others. "Benches and sculptures over by those trees."

Shane and Dean grabbed a toppled bench and hauled it over to the grassy area. Lauren carried a soot-streaked metal sculpture. Riley and Larry picked up a second bench, which was missing two slats.

"Hey, Riley, I brought a snack," Larry said as they carried the bench.

"Great." Riley scanned the garden, thinking ahead. After this, they'd clear out any dead bushes. Do some trimming. Then start on the flower beds.

"I brought enough for you, too," Larry said.

"Thanks, Larry." Riley set down her end of the bench and started back toward another overturned sculpture. Power saw, she thought. Don't forget to get one. From somewhere...

Larry hurried alongside her. "I've got rice cakes and mango juice," he said, keeping pace. "Trail mix and—"

Lauren got to the sculpture before Riley, so Riley swerved toward another toppled bench and crashed into Larry.

"—Chips Ahoy!" Larry staggered backward. "Hey, you really like those, right?"

"Huh? Sorry, Larry," Riley said. "I've just got so much on my mind now, I guess I wasn't listening." This could be a problem, she thought. Larry wasn't *trying* to get in her way, but he definitely was. "Hey, Larry, I have a project for you," she said.

"Sure!" Larry said eagerly. "You're the boss, Riley. What do you want me to do?"

"Like Mr. Watkins said, most of the benches are going to need work," Riley told him. "It would be great if you could pry off the broken slats and figure out how much wood we'll need."

"No problem. I'm on it." Larry turned away, then stopped. "Hey, Riley, want to get pizza with me when we're done for the day?"

[**Riley: Uh-oh. This could be another problem. It's what's known as WYGOWM, short for "Will You Go Out With Me?" It's sort of a game Larry and I play. The rules are simple, and the ending is always the same: He asks me out. I say...**]

"No, Larry," Riley said.

Larry grinned. "Just checking."

"Larry!" Shane called from across the garden. He pointed to a slab of marble lying on the ground. "Come give me and Dean a hand with this thing—it weighs a ton!"

"Muscle Man to the rescue!" Larry called. "I'll do the benches next, Riley. Then I'll be back!"

That's what I'm afraid of, Riley thought as she watched Larry trot across the trampled garden. It's not that she wasn't used to him hanging around and asking her out. He'd had a crush on her for years. But now she was in charge of this huge project, and she had to prove she could handle it.

And she couldn't do that with Larry being lovesick all the time.... If only he'd find someone else to ask out.

chapter two

Chloe's stomach did a little flip when her father pulled up in front of the Sunnyview Retirement Home. The place was a lot closer to her house than she'd thought. And she was starting to get nervous!

"Thanks for the ride, Dad," she said. "I can walk home later." She gave Jake a quick kiss on the cheek, but she didn't get out of the car.

"Okay, honey." Jake waited a second. "Chloe? Aren't you going in?"

"Actually, I feel a little weird about this," Chloe admitted. "I mean, what am I going to do with these people? There's such a generation gap. We have nothing in common. What will we talk about?"

Jake smiled. "Just be yourself. Older people aren't aliens—you'll have plenty to talk about."

Like what? Chloe wondered, getting out of the car. They won't care about stuff like hot clothes or the latest coffee flavor at Starbucks. But as she walked up to the apartment building, she gave herself a pep talk. Be positive. After all, you'll be helping somebody out. And you're getting extra credit. Community service will look great on your college application. So what if you won't be applying for another three years?

Chloe walked past two flower-filled planters and pulled open the front door.

Quinn Reyes, one of Chloe's friends from school, was sitting on one of the chairs inside the roomy lobby, talking on her cell phone. Another friend, Amanda Gray, was checking out the huge bulletin board hanging on one of the walls.

Chloe waved to Quinn and hurried over to Amanda. "Hi, Amanda! I didn't know you'd signed up for this."

"I didn't know *you* did," Amanda said.

"It was sort of a last-minute thing," Chloe told her. She glanced around. Two elderly women crossed the lobby and stopped at the mailboxes on the other side of the room. A man and a woman moved slowly toward the front doors. "So what are we supposed to do?" she asked. "Just grab somebody and ask if they need anything?"

Amanda tucked her brown hair behind her ears and laughed. "Not exactly. When Mrs. Carpenter—she's the director of Sunnyview—came to talk to us at school, she said she'd introduce us to the people who signed up for the program. I don't see her yet, so I guess we wait."

Amanda headed for one of the chairs. As Chloe started to follow her, she brushed against the bulletin board. A Chinese take-out menu fluttered to the floor. Chloe grabbed it and stuck it back on.

The bulletin board was almost totally covered: more take-out menus, senior-citizen hot-line numbers, bus schedules, symphony and museum brochures, and a "Sunnyview Birthday List."

As she checked out some of the notices, Chloe heard footsteps behind her. She turned.

A boy stood a couple of feet away. Gray eyes, curly dark hair, and a crooked little smile that made him look as if he'd just heard a private joke.

Cute, Chloe thought. Very cute. She'd seen him before. He was a transfer student at West Malibu High. She didn't know his name, but she could definitely think of a few things to say to *him*. Maybe Sunnyview had flirting potential after all!

Chloe gave herself a quick, mental once-over. Too bad she'd worn such blah clothes. But at least she had on her cute accessories—her favorite turquoise choker and hand-beaded bracket. "Hi," she said with a smile.

"Hey," he said. He moved closer and leaned next to the bulletin board. "I'm Lennon Porter."

"Chloe Carlson," she told him. "I've seen you around school." His eyes weren't totally gray, Chloe noticed. There was blue in them, too. They looked really cool with the dark hair.

"Me, too. I mean, I've seen you, too." He grinned. "Actually, I've seen two of you."

Chloe laughed. "You must have seen me with Riley, my sister. We're twins."

"Right. I figured that out pretty fast," he said. "So you're Chloe," he added.

Chloe nodded. "Yup." She loved the way he kept looking at her.

"So let me guess," Lennon said. "You're here to do your part as a good citizen of Malibu."

"You mean the community service thing? Right," Chloe agreed.

Lennon nodded. "That's what I figured, since I haven't seen you here before."

"What do you mean? Are you visiting your grandparents or something?" Chloe asked. "I thought you were a volunteer, too."

"I am. But I've been working here ever since I moved back to Malibu."

"Back?" Chloe repeated.

"Yeah," Lennon said. "I used to live here. When I was a kid my mom moved us to Japan for business. Then India. Then Italy."

"Really? I'm impressed," Chloe said.

Lennon shrugged. "No big deal."

"Well, I've barely been out of California," Chloe admitted. "My parents took me and my sister to the Grand Canyon once. It was cool." And so is he, she thought. Not to mention totally hot! "So, what do you do here?" she asked, trying to sound casual.

"I do stuff for Mrs. Scanlon and Mrs. Davidson," Lennon told her. "They're widows. Also cousins, and they share an apartment. It's fun. I like it."

"You do?" Chloe knew she sounded surprised, but she couldn't help it. How could spending so much time at a retirement home be fun?

Lennon smiled. "A lot of kids don't like it—but they sign up because it looks good on their college applications. Don't worry," he added softly, "I won't tell anybody that's why *you're* here."

"That's...that's *not* the reason I volunteered!" Chloe sputtered, even though it kind of was. "Why did you say that?"

"Because of your outfit," he said.

"My outfit?" Chloe said. "What's the matter with it?"

He shrugged. "Nothing. Except you don't dress like that at school. It's obvious you're wearing your 'old folks' clothes. It's like you're playing a part. You aren't serious about this."

Chloe felt her cheeks burn. Who did this Lennon guy think he was? Okay, so maybe she wasn't thrilled about being there. And maybe she was kind of glad to get the extra credit. But that didn't mean she couldn't be serious about volunteering. Just because he'd been all over the world didn't mean he knew *everything*.

"You are so totally wrong," Chloe declared. "I happen

to think that community service is very, *very* important!"

"Really?" Lennon's mouth curled up in that "private joke" smile. No, not a smile. A smirk, Chloe decided. "So what else have you done?" he asked.

Chloe thought a second. She'd collected cans of soup and stuff in the Cans for Cambodia Food Drive back in seventh grade, but that was about it. It wasn't much. If she told him, he'd probably laugh.

"Well?" Lennon asked.

Chloe scowled at him. "Why should I bother telling *you*?"

"Hey, whatever," Lennon said. Still smirking, he pushed away from the wall and walked over to the two women at the mailboxes. "Hey, Mrs. S! Mrs. D! What's on for today?"

The women greeted him with big smiles. "We're ready for anything," one of them said. "Let's go into the lounge and plan something exciting!"

Quinn sped over to Chloe's side. "Ooh, he's cute!" she said, snapping her phone shut. Her dark eyes sparkled. "Who is he?"

"Lennon Porter," Chloe said, gritting her teeth. "But don't let the cute part fool you. He's totally rude!"

"Hey, you guys," Amanda called out. "Mrs. Carpenter's here. We're supposed to go into the lounge."

Chloe and Quinn followed Amanda into the big lounge off the lobby. Lennon, Mrs. S, and Mrs. D were already ahead. The two women had linked arms with

Lennon and were laughing at something he'd said. They obviously thought he was incredibly charming.

Chloe rolled her eyes. He definitely had the cousins fooled.

"Welcome, everyone." Mrs. Carpenter, a slender, middle-aged woman, stood in the center of the lounge and smiled as Chloe and the others entered. "Thank you so much for volunteering your time. It means a lot to us, and we're sure you'll find it rewarding as well."

Chloe glanced around. The lounge was a large room with comfortable furniture, a television, two computers, and shelves filled with books, decks of cards, and board games. Colorful prints decorated the walls.

Lennon sat on one of the couches with the cousins. Two more women were sitting by the computers. Mrs. Carpenter introduced Amanda to one—Mrs. Lowe—and Quinn to the other—Mrs. Steiner. Then she walked over to Chloe. "Let's see, you must be Chloe," she said, checking the list on her clipboard.

Chloe smiled and nodded.

"I've matched you with Mr. Simms." Mrs. Carpenter pointed. "He's over there, behind the ficus tree."

Looking across the room, Chloe spotted an elderly, balding man sitting in a chair half hidden by a leafy potted plant. His head was bent over a newspaper and a wooden cane lay across his knees.

Beep, beep, beep, beep.

"Oops, there goes my beeper." Mrs. Carpenter

pulled a black beeper from her belt and checked the number. "Oh, dear, I should return this call right away. You go ahead and introduce yourself, Chloe. I'll be back in a few minutes."

Okay, here goes, Chloe thought nervously, walking across the room. Be cheerful. Be friendly. And prove to Lennon that you're serious about this! She stopped near the chair. "Hi, Mr. Simms!" she said in her chirpy voice. "I'm Chloe Carlson!"

Mr. Simms didn't even glance up from the paper.

He must be hard of hearing, Chloe decided. She cleared her throat. "HI, MR. SIMMS!" she almost shouted. "I'M CHLOE CARLSON!"

Mr. Simms jumped, rattling the paper and scowling at her from beneath his thick white eyebrows. "No need to shout, young lady. I use a cane, not a hearing aid."

Chloe could feel her cheeks flush. What an embarrassing mistake! She glanced around.

Lennon was smirking at her. No one else was even looking. He *would* be the only one who noticed, she thought.

She frowned at him and turned back to Mr. Simms. "I'm sorry. I didn't mean to shout," she said. "Anyway, I'm Chloe."

Mr. Simms nodded. "Yep. I heard that loud and clear."

"So…is there anything special you want to do today?" Chloe asked.

"Nope," Mr. Simms replied with a shrug.

Oh, great. Chloe thought she was supposed to do whatever *he* wanted. Now she had to come up with some ideas. She glanced around again. Lennon caught her eye and grinned.

Chloe gritted her teeth. Lennon was obviously waiting for her to mess up. Or quit. Well, no way would she give him the satisfaction.

Chloe put on a big smile and turned back to Mr. Simms again. "Well!" she said brightly. Well what? she wondered. What am I going to do with him?

Slightly panicked, she looked around again. Lennon and the two ladies were on their way out. Quinn and Mrs. Steiner were leaving, too. Amanda and Mrs. Lowe were at one of the computers.

That gave Chloe an idea. If she could get Mr. Simms in front of a computer, they might find something to talk about. Plus they could kill lots of time.

"The second computer is free," Chloe said. "If you don't know how to use it, I could show you. You can shop and e-mail people and—"

"I can use a computer," Mr. Simms interrupted. "Don't much like it."

"Oh." So much for that, Chloe thought. "Well, how about cards?" she suggested, spotting a card table in one corner of the room.

"Only good game is poker," Mr Simms declared. "Not enough people here for that."

"Scrabble? Monopoly? Backgammon?" Chloe asked,

feeling a little desperate. Why did Mr. Simms sign up for this, anyway? "Television? Books? I could read something to you. Not that I think your eyesight's bad or anything," she quickly added, hoping she hadn't insulted him again.

"I'm seventy-eight years old! My eyesight's terrible!"

Oookay, Chloe thought. This guy was such a grump! Too bad she couldn't tell him so. She had to be nice no matter what. She took another deep breath. "So would you like me to read you something?" she asked sweetly.

Mr. Simms shrugged. "I could stand it."

"Great!" Chloe gave a little sigh of relief. "What do you like?"

Another shrug.

"Not a problem!" Chloe said, keeping her voice extra cheerful. "I'll read out some titles and you tell me what sounds good."

Crossing to the bookshelves, Chloe knelt down and checked out some of the titles. "There's a bunch of history," she called over her shoulder. "World War I, World War II, lots of stuff on California—"

"Dry as dust," Mr. Simms declared.

Be nice, Chloe reminded herself. Keep sounding friendly. She scooted down the shelf. "How about poetry?"

"Ha!" Mr. Simms cried.

I'll take that as a no, Chloe decided. She searched the shelves. "Here's a whole set of Mark Twain and one of Willa Cather. And Charles Dickens."

Mr. Simms said nothing, so Chloe kept searching. "Romance, adventure...oh, and mysteries! That could be fun."

No answer.

Chloe puffed out a breath. She had to find *something* he liked. "Cookbooks...self-help...biographies. Do you like biographies?"

Still no answer.

Maybe he didn't really want to be read to, Chloe thought. After all, he hadn't exactly jumped up and down when she'd suggested it. She'd have to think of something else to do.

"Maybe reading wasn't such a good idea," Chloe said.

But when she turned around, Mr. Simms wasn't in his chair anymore. In fact, he wasn't even in the lounge!

I can't believe this, Chloe said to herself. He totally left!

She had a feeling that her time at Sunnyview was going to pass very slowly.

chapter
three

This is so humiliating, Chloe thought. Where did he go? Why did he go? Hadn't she acted nice and friendly even though he was grouchy?

Chloe crossed the lounge and peered into the lobby. Mr. Simms wasn't there, so she went over to the computer desk. "Amanda, did you see Mr. Simms leave?"

Amanda and Mrs. Lowe glanced up from the computer. They both shook their heads. "We haven't come up for air since we logged on to eBay," Amanda explained.

Mrs. Lowe smiled. "It's my first visit. I'm just about ready to bid on an antique necklace."

Chloe went back to the lobby. Mr. Simms couldn't have gotten far, could he? She glanced around, spotted the mailboxes, and hurried over to them. She was searching for his apartment number when Mrs. Carpenter came out of her office.

"I'm sorry I took so long with that phone call, Chloe," the director said. "How are you and Mr. Simms getting along?"

We're not, Chloe thought. "I'm not sure," she said. "Actually, he, uh…" She hesitated. It would sound really bad if she admitted she'd lost him.

Fortunately the phone rang in Mrs. Carpenter's office. With an apologetic smile, she spun around and hurried to answer it.

Chloe turned to the mailboxes again. Simms… Simms…there it was. H. Simms. Apartment 81. She'd go check it out. If he wasn't there, then she'd tell Mrs. Carpenter. After all, Mr. Simms *was* kind of old. He could have fallen down or gotten sick or something. She should have thought of that in the first place.

She hurried down one of the halls lined with apartment doors, found Number 81, and rang the bell. "Mr. Simms?" she called. She rang the bell again and waited.

No answer.

Worried now, Chloe ran back to the lobby.

Lennon and the cousins were just coming through the front doors. "Have you seen Mr. Simms?" Chloe asked breathlessly.

Lennon cocked an eyebrow. "What did you do to the poor man?"

"Nothing!" Chloe protested. "He left when I wasn't looking!"

"Don't worry, dear. Harry probably went into the

sunroom," one of the women said. "I'm Mrs. Scanlon, by the way. Come on, let's go see if he's there."

Mrs. Scanlon, Mrs. Davidson, and Lennon set off across the lobby. Chloe kept her fingers crossed and hurried along with them.

"So, what do you think of Harry?" Mrs. Davidson asked Chloe.

"Well…" Chloe hesitated again. She didn't want to say what she *really* thought of him.

Mrs. Davidson laughed. "I know. He's a real grump! Has been for years. It's a pity—I've heard he used to be a real ladies' man, always out dancing and going to lots of parties."

"Are we talking about the same Mr. Simms?" Chloe asked.

"A younger Mr. Simms," Mrs. Scanlon said. "I didn't know him then, but supposedly he was a charmer. Hard to believe, isn't it?"

Impossible, Chloe thought.

"You were right, Mrs. S," Lennon said. He pointed through a doorway. "There he is."

Chloe looked into a bright, screened-in room with huge potted plants and cushioned patio furniture on the tiled floor.

Mr. Simms was stretched out on a recliner, snoring gently.

Chloe couldn't believe it. He'd sneaked away from her to take a nap! Talk about embarrassing! Chloe was tempted to quit this whole thing. She was no good at it. And Mr. Simms obviously wouldn't care. He'd probably wake up and cheer.

Lennon nudged Chloe in the arm. "Nice job, Chloe," he murmured, giving her one of his irritating grins. "Looks like you bored him to sleep."

"Thanks, Lennon!" Chloe said with a big fake smile. She took a deep breath and headed into the sunroom.

If Lennon-the-Perfect thought she couldn't handle this, he had another thing coming. She'd prove she was as good at this as he was. Scratch that—she'd prove she was *better*!

Riley surveyed the library garden. Phase One of her plan—clearing away everything that needed cleaning or fixing—was almost finished. Looking good! she thought as she wiped her forehead.

"You look hot, Riley," Larry said, speeding over from the group of broken benches. "Want to take a break? I brought mango juice, remember?"

"Thanks, Larry, but not yet," Riley told him. She *was* kind of thirsty, but it was way too soon for a break. "I want to get started on the bushes and the flower beds." That was Phase Two of her plan—raking the beds, trimming the bushes that could be saved, and pulling up the dead ones.

"Come on, let's help Shane and Lauren with the bricks," Riley said. Unfortunately, most of the bricks edging the flower beds were broken and needed to be cleared.

Note to self, Riley thought as she and Larry walked over to one of the flower beds. Find out where to get bricks.

"Hey, Riley, what happened to Dean?" Shane called from the next flower bed, where he and Lauren were pulling up chunks of brick.

"He had basketball practice," Riley told him. Note to self number two: Call Dean and remind him to bring his dad's power saw tomorrow. What else? she wondered. She hadn't expected to be in charge, and it was getting hard to keep everything in her head. She'd have to make out a schedule when she got home. That would keep things on track. Maybe she'd even show it to Mr. Watkins so he'd see that she knew what she was doing.

"I can't believe Dean left so soon," Lauren grumbled. "This place is still such a mess!"

"It won't look that way for long," Riley declared. "All we have to do is keep working and it'll be gorgeous. You'll see."

Riley reached for a chunk of brick. Larry bent down for it at the same time. Riley quickly changed course and started looking for another one. In two seconds, Larry was at her side again.

Riley sighed. He's not trying to get in my way, she reminded herself. He just *is*.

"Hey, Riley," Larry said, tossing a piece of brick from

hand to hand. "Instead of pizza after we finish, want to get—whoa!" The brick flew from his hands and landed on Riley's foot. "Oops. Sorry, Riley."

"It's okay." Good thing I'm wearing boots, she thought as she tossed the chunk of brick into a pile. And Larry's not trying to be clumsy. He just *is*.

"Listen, Larry, why don't you do that side of the flower bed and I'll do this side?" Riley suggested, pointing to the other end. At least he'll be out of my way, she thought. And maybe he'll forget about asking me out for a while. "We'll work toward the middle and get it done faster."

"You're the boss!" Larry agreed. As he brought his hand up in a salute, he accidentally hit Riley on the chin.

"Oh, sorry!" he said. "You okay?"

"Fine," Riley assured him. Which was a lie. Larry was starting to get on her nerves. She had a lot of stuff on her mind. How could she think with him hanging over her all the time?

Tonight I'll come up with another project for him, she decided. One that will keep him really, really busy.

With Larry on the other side of the flower bed, Riley was able to work more quickly. Shane and Lauren worked fast, too, and the pile of broken bricks grew higher and higher.

"I think that's the last of them," Lauren said. She tossed a chunk onto the pile and dusted her hands.

"Great!" Riley said, wiping her forehead again. "Now we can start trimming and raking and then we'll really see a major change!"

"Are you sure you don't want to take a break, Riley?" Larry asked. "Have a drink of mango juice."

"Yuck." Lauren made a gagging sound. "I hate that stuff."

Riley was beginning to hate it, too, mainly because Larry kept bugging her to have some. What was she going to do about him?

"Let's keep going," Riley said. "I mean, sure, get a drink. But I really want to work on the flower beds and the bushes before we take a real break. We might not be able to finish today because the bricks took longer than I thought. But at least we can get started."

"You're the boss!" Larry agreed. Hoisting a rake over his shoulder, he marched into one of the churned-up flower beds.

Lauren went to work on a second one. Shane and Riley began clipping some bushes that lined one of the paths.

"You know what we need?" Shane asked.

"Wooden slats for the benches," Riley said, thinking ahead. "Paint for the wooden slats. Flowers—"

"No, music," Shane interrupted, clipping off a broken branch. "I'll bring my boom box Monday."

"Cool. Wait!" Riley stared at him. "What do you mean, Monday? Won't you be here tomorrow?"

Tomorrow was Saturday. They wouldn't be working on Sunday.

Shane shook his head. "Gotta go visit my grand-parents."

Riley nodded. She could hardly tell him to forget his grandparents. But tomorrow she'd planned to finish the trimming and stuff they didn't get done today. Then while she and Larry and Lauren got the flower beds ready, she was going to have Shane and Dean cut the new slats for the benches.

I'll just help with the slats instead, she decided. No big deal. And maybe I'll stay longer today, just so we don't fall behind.

"Hey, everybody!" George Watkins rounded the corner of the library. "How's it going? Any problems?"

"No, everything's great," Riley said. "No problems at all." Well, maybe a couple, she thought. But she wasn't going to tell Mr. Watkins. He'd probably want to take over or something, and she knew she could handle this.

George glanced around. "What happened to Dean?"

"He had to leave. But he'll be here tomorrow," Riley assured him.

George nodded. "Okay, good. The dirt will be here then, too."

Dirt? Riley wondered. Why do they need more dirt? They've got lots of it!

"It's nice, rich soil," George continued. "Good for flowers."

"Thanks!" Riley said. Oh, *that* kind of dirt, she thought.

"Of course, they'll just dump the bags of the stuff in a big pile," George added. "You'll need to put it into the beds and rake it out."

"Of course," Riley agreed. She was definitely staying longer today.

"So…" George glanced around again. "It looks as if you've got things under control out here. See you later."

"Later, Mr. Watkins," Riley said. Okay, so she hadn't thought of the dirt. So what? It wouldn't take that long to shovel it into the flower beds, would it?

But we definitely can't waste any time, Riley thought after George left. We only have a week. Every minute counts. She grabbed a twisted branch on one of the bushes. "Oww!"

Shane glanced up. "I forgot to warn you—some of these bushes have thorns."

"No kidding." Riley checked her hand. There were several drops of bright red blood on her palm.

Larry immediately appeared at her side. "Are you okay?" he asked. "What happened?"

"Attack of the thorns," Shane said.

"Let me see," Larry insisted. "Ooh, blood!"

"Just a little," Riley said, wiping her palm on her overalls.

"How come you weren't wearing your gloves?" Larry demanded. "Want a Band-Aid? George left a first-aid kit. I could kiss it to make it better…."

"No, Larry," Riley replied. "It's okay. Really."

"Riley, what should we do next?" Lauren asked. Shane was behind her.

"I think we should quit for the day," Larry said. "Riley's hurt."

"I am *not* hurt, Larry," Riley said.

"Are you sure?" Larry asked.

"Yes!" Riley cried. She wished he would stop hovering. She totally lost her concentration. She couldn't even think of the next step. "Maybe we should take a break," she told Lauren.

"I'm all about taking a break," Shane agreed.

"Okay," Riley said. "Ten minutes."

Shane stabbed his clippers into the dirt and headed toward the shade trees at the far end of the garden.

Larry grinned at Riley. "I'll get the mango juice!"

As Larry sped off, Riley sighed. She had to do something about him—fast!

She spotted Sierra Pomeroy rounding the back corner of the library. Sierra was one of Riley's best friends.

"Hey, Sierra!" Riley cried, hurrying across the dirt. "What are you doing here?"

"I'm on my way to band practice," Sierra said, shaking back her long, wavy red hair. She and some other kids—including Riley's boyfriend, Alex—had started a band called The Wave. "I figured I'd stop to see how you're...hey! Overalls!"

"Huh?" Riley glanced down at herself.

"Your overalls—they just gave me an idea!" Sierra said excitedly. "I could get some and wear my cool out-fits under them. It would cut minutes off my changing time!"

Riley laughed. Sierra's parents didn't approve of cool clothes like low-rise jeans or cropped tops. So Sierra kept some in her locker and changed when she got to school. "What about tops?" she asked. "Overalls just have straps."

Sierra frowned. "Okay, that's a problem. Skirts, too, I guess."

Larry trotted up and handed a can of mango juice to Riley. "Hi, Sierra," he said.

Sierra smiled. "Hi, Larry."

Riley groaned to herself. He was back so soon! And she needed to talk to Sierra about him. Cancel that—she needed to *complain* to Sierra about him.

"Here, Sierra, you take this," Riley said, holding out the can of juice. "You said you were thirsty after walking all this way, right?"

"Uh…" Sierra said.

"Right?" Riley repeated, swiveling her eyes to Larry.

"Sure. Right!" Sierra took the juice. "Thanks, Larry."

"No problem. I'll get you another one, Riley." Larry sped off again.

Riley sighed. "Larry is driving me nuts!" she declared. "He won't leave me alone."

Sierra grinned. "This is new? He's had a crush on you since kindergarten."

"I know, but this time it's different," Riley said. "This garden is a super-big deal. And I'm the one in charge."

"Whoa," Sierra said.

Riley nodded. "I know I can handle it, but I have a million things to think about. And I can't take a step without bumping into Larry. He brought snacks for me and asked me out for pizza later. I got stuck with a thorn and he was ready to perform CPR!"

Sierra laughed. "Come on, he's just trying to help. I think it's kind of sweet."

[<u>Riley</u>: See the lightbulb over my head? See how it just went on? That's because I suddenly had a brilliant idea!]

"Sierra, you have to help me," Riley said. "Please say yes. Please, please!"

"Say yes to what?" Sierra asked.

"Well, you like Larry," Riley reminded her. "I mean, as a friend, right?"

"Well, sure," Sierra agreed. "He's a nice guy."

Riley nodded eagerly. "So if he asked you out, would you go?"

Sierra stared at her in surprise. "Me?"

Riley quickly glanced across the garden. Larry had stopped to talk to Lauren and Shane. She had a little time. "If Larry went on a date with somebody, then maybe he wouldn't pay so much attention to me. And I could concentrate on the garden. So will you?"

"Me?" Sierra asked again. "Go out with Larry?"

"Please, please!" Riley begged. "I know it's a huge favor, but I'm desperate!" She glanced at Larry again. He was heading toward them.

"Well, okay," Sierra agreed.

"Thank you!" Riley cried. "Thank you, thank you!"

"No problem. Of course, he has to ask me," Sierra added.

"Don't worry, I'll take care of that!" Riley said. Then she crossed her fingers and hoped she could make it happen.

chapter
four

"And you'll bring the power saw, right?" Riley reminded Dean on the phone that evening. "Your dad's okay with it? Great! See you tomorrow."

Riley hung up. "It's a good thing I called him," she told Chloe, who was standing in front of their bedroom mirror, getting ready to go to a movie. "He didn't think we'd be working tomorrow."

"Well, tomorrow *is* Saturday." Chloe rubbed on some pearl-pink lip gloss.

"I know. But it's not like we have forever to get this done." Riley picked up a pad of paper and checked the schedule she'd made. She had stayed late today, but the trimming still wasn't finished. They'd do that in the morning. It wouldn't take long. Then they'd shovel the dirt into the flower beds and work on the benches.

"Wood!" she cried. "I measured the benches, but I

totally forgot to call the lumberyard to order the wood!"

"You can do it first thing in the morning," Chloe said.

"Right, that's plenty of time." Riley made a note and underlined it three times. She scanned the schedule again. Had she forgotten anything else? She didn't think so. "So far, so good," she said. "I can't wait to get started tomorrow!"

Chloe groaned. "I wish I could say that. Unfortunately I'll be seeing Lennon Porter again."

Riley had heard all about the Sunnyview fiasco. "Can't you just ignore him?"

"Impossible," Chloe said. "He keeps pointing out everything I'm doing wrong. And to think I actually thought he was *cute* when I first met him!" She picked up a brush and ran it through her hair. "Ugh! I'd love to wipe that smirky grin off his face! It's a big challenge, but somebody's got to do it."

"You think *that's* a challenge?" Riley joined Chloe at the mirror and put on some blush. The Wave was performing tonight and she had to get going. "I have to set Larry up with Sierra."

Chloe stared at her. "Larry and S*ierra*?"

Riley quickly explained her plan.

"It'll never happen," Chloe declared. "Larry's in love with *you*."

"Yeah, but I have to try," Riley argued. "If he starts seeing somebody else, he might realize that we're just friends. Just think—he could actually get over me. And

I'm putting the plan in motion tonight, so wish me luck!"

"Luck!" Chloe called as Riley grabbed her jacket and headed out the door.

Riley left the house and hurried to California Dream, a popular beach club and hangout. It was where The Wave had had their first big gig. They had been a big hit, and the club kept asking them back.

When Riley arrived, the band was already on the deck that jutted out onto the sand. Saul, the drummer, kept the beat while Marta did riffs on her keyboard. Alex and Sierra were tuning their guitars.

Alex was a quiet guy with sandy brown hair and dark brown eyes. When he caught sight of Riley, he stopped tuning up and walked to the edge of the deck. "Hey," he said, smiling.

Riley's heart gave a funny little thump, the way it always did when he smiled at her. "Hi. It looks like you guys are getting a good crowd."

"Yeah, it's great," he agreed. "And you're here, that's what really matters."

Riley's heart gave a double thump.

"I'd better get ready," Alex said. He leaned down and gave Riley a quick kiss. "I'll see you after, okay?"

"Definitely," Riley said. She watched him walk back toward Sierra. Then she scanned the crowd. Good, there was Larry, walking straight toward her. Time to put her plan into action.

"Hi, Riley!" Larry said. "I knew you'd be here!"

so little time

[Riley: And I knew he knew, so I knew he'd be here, too! That was the easy part of the plan. Now for the tricky part.]

"Want to sit with me?" Larry asked.

"Sure," Riley agreed.

Larry looked startled. "You do?"

"Yes—come on, let's find a space." Riley led him through the gathering crowd to a spot with a good view of the deck. "This is perfect," she said, plopping down in the sand. "I like to be close, especially when Sierra's singing."

"Yeah, she's fun to watch," Larry said, settling down next to Riley.

"Sierra is so amazingly talented!" Riley added. "First violin in the school orchestra, bass guitar in The Wave— plus she can sing!"

Larry nodded and looked at Sierra.

Riley looked at her, too. Sierra wore black jeans, a tight red tank top, and glitter in her wavy hair. "Sierra looks really pretty tonight, doesn't she?"

"She always looks pretty," Larry said. "Hey, Riley, want to get something to eat with me after the show?"

"Umm…" Riley thought fast. She had to keep his mind on Sierra. "I'm probably going somewhere with Alex."

"Okay. What about tomorrow?" Larry asked. "After we finish at the garden, we could—"

"Larry, wait," she said. "You know why I keep saying no when you ask me out, don't you? It's because of Alex. I mean, he's my boyfriend. But you know what?"

"What?" Larry asked.

"I think you should ask Sierra out," Riley told him.

Larry's eyebrows rose. "You do?"

Riley nodded. "She likes you. I bet she'll say yes."

"Well…" Larry looked at Sierra on the stage. "Okay."

Well, that was easy, Riley thought.

The band launched into its first number—a loud, bass-heavy tune that got the crowd dancing in the sand.

Riley jumped up and danced with everyone else. This is so perfect, she thought. If I can keep Larry off my back for a little while, I'll be able to concentrate on the garden!

She glanced at Larry, who was clapping and smiling up at Sierra on the stage. He hadn't taken his eyes off her for a second. Riley shook her head. Boy, he sure got over me fast!

This could be it, Chloe thought, standing at the Sunnyview bulletin board on Saturday afternoon. She carefully reread one of the notices. This could be the perfect thing for Mr. Simms and me to do together.

"Chloe Carlson!" Lennon Porter called out as he came into the lobby. "You're back!"

"Of course I'm back," Chloe declared, turning from the bulletin board. "Don't sound so surprised. Did you think I was going to quit or something?"

"Did I sound surprised?" Lennon asked her. "Maybe it's because I see you're not wearing your 'old folks' clothes today."

Chloe looked down at her pink Capri pants and white cotton top and rolled her eyes. Okay, so she'd decided to dress normally. But she'd never admit to Lennon that he had anything to do with it.

"Anyway, all I really meant was I'm glad to see you," Lennon told her.

"Oh." Chloe eyed him suspiciously. "Well," she said. "Where are the cousins?"

"In their apartment, I guess. I'm going to help them paint their living room," Lennon explained. "So what do you have planned with Mr. Simms?"

"I have to talk to him first," Chloe said. "But I was just looking at the bulletin board and I remembered what Mrs. Scanlon said yesterday—that Mr. Simms used to like parties and dancing. So I'm going to tell him about this." Chloe tapped the notice.

Lennon peered at it. "A dance at the senior citizens center?"

Chloe nodded. "This afternoon. And the center is only a couple of blocks from here. It's a good idea, isn't it?"

"Yeah, it's a great idea," he agreed.

"Thanks," Chloe said. She liked the little twinkle in his eyes when he smiled. And he liked her idea. This was getting off to a very good start. Maybe Lennon wasn't so bad, after all.

"Except..." Lennon added.

I should have known, Chloe thought. "Except what?" she asked.

"Except that Mr. Simms uses a cane all the time," Lennon reminded her. "Dancing might be tough for him."

[Chloe: Don't you hate it when a know-it-all is right? It's too humiliating to agree with them, but you have to say something!]

"I think I'll let Mr. Simms decide," Chloe replied.

"Yeah, sure." Lennon's eyes lit up as his smirk came back. "I mean, what do I know? You're the expert on senior citizens," he said and headed down the hall toward the apartments.

Chloe stood there and fumed for a second. Why couldn't she ever think of a good comeback? And why did he have to be so cute!

As she walked across the lobby, Amanda and Quinn and their senior citizens came out of the lounge. "Hi, you guys," Chloe said. "Is Mr. Simms in there?"

Amanda nodded. "But I think he might be asleep."

"He's always catnapping," Mrs. Lowe said.

Great, Chloe thought. Would she have to wake him up? "Where are you guys going?" she asked.

"Shopping," Quinn said. "Want to come? There's a special bus that goes to the malls and supermarkets and everything."

Mrs. Steiner nodded. "It should be here any minute, so we're going to wait outside."

"Oh. Okay," Chloe said. "Maybe I'll see you out there." She hurried toward the lounge, trying to decide.

Shopping or dancing? Was Mr. Simms a mall kind of guy? He didn't seem like it, but it wouldn't hurt to ask. Maybe she shouldn't suggest dancing, even though she hated taking Lennon's advice. She didn't want Mr. Simms to think she was totally insensitive.

Chloe found Mr. Simms sitting in the same chair as yesterday, half hidden by the ficus tree. "Hi, Mr. Simms!" she said in her most cheerful tone. "How are you?"

Mr. Simms peered up at her. "You're back."

Chloe groaned to herself. He sounded surprised, just like Lennon had. Well, she'd show *him*, too. "Sure I'm back!" she said in her "happy voice." "And it's such a beautiful, sunny day, I—"

"It's supposed to cloud up tonight," he interrupted.

"Okay, but that's tonight!" Chloe said. "It's beautiful now. So why don't we take the bus and—"

"Too late," he interrupted again.

Chloe frowned. "Huh?"

Mr. Simms jerked a thumb over his shoulder. Chloe glanced out the window in time to see the mall bus pull away.

"Oookay, I guess that's out," Chloe said, laughing way too hard. Now what? she wondered. No way would she suggest reading again. He'd said no to cards and the computer yesterday, so doing those things were out, too.

But walking wasn't. He'd sneaked away from her fast enough yesterday. He could definitely move.

"How about some fresh air?" she suggested brightly. "The beach is only a block away. We can walk along the boardwalk."

Mr. Simms thumped his cane on the floor and stood up. "Fresh air couldn't hurt."

"Great!" Chloe cried, relieved. She'd finally come up with something!

Mr. Simms wasn't all that slow, even with the cane, and soon they were at the boardwalk. It was crowded with people and lined with stands selling everything from art to ice cream to flip-flops and T-shirts.

"The ocean smells awesome!" Chloe said, taking a deep breath. "It always makes me hungry. What about you, Mr. Simms? Do you want a hot dog or something?"

"Those things will kill you," he muttered, maneuvering his way through the crowd.

Chloe kept smiling, even though her cheeks were beginning to ache. "A tofu dog then," she said. "Or fruit? I see a stand up there with fresh fruit."

"Let's just walk," he said. "It's nice. Pretty as a picture out here. I used to take a lot of pictures."

[Chloe: Did you hear that? He said it's pretty. It's not exactly a major breakthrough, but maybe he's starting to thaw out a little!]

"It *is* pretty," Chloe agreed. "My house is on the beach, and I can walk along it anytime. I guess I sort of take it for granted sometimes."

"Mmm," Mr. Simms grunted. "Well, everybody takes things for granted sometimes. You've just got to remember to take time out to enjoy the little things in life. The sky, the flowers, the ocean…and hey, they're usually free!"

"You're right!" Chloe laughed. They were actually having a conversation, and she liked it. It was nice to see that Mr. Simms wasn't always a grouchy person. Maybe he had just had something on his mind before.

Chloe thought for a minute. Maybe I should even mention the senior citizens dance. We could go another time.

"You know what I like to do besides walk?" Chloe said. "I like to dance."

Mr. Simms glanced at her.

Is that the beginning of a smile? Chloe wondered. Or is his mouth just crooked? "What about you, Mr. Simms?" she asked. "Do you like—"

"Heads up!" someone shouted.

Chloe gasped. A pack of in-line skaters were swarming down the boardwalk. And she and Mr. Simms were right in their path! "Get to the side!" she urged him. "Fast!"

Chloe grabbed Mr. Simms's elbow and pulled him toward the side of the boardwalk. "Hurry!" she cried. She gave Mr. Simms an extra-hard tug. They stumbled onto a bench as the skaters zoomed by.

"That was close," Chloe said. "I can't believe they didn't even stop! Are you okay, Mr. Simms?"

Mr. Simms nodded. "Shouldn't have come," he grumbled. "It's too dangerous out here for an old man with a cane."

"That's not true," Chloe said. "Anyway, they're gone."

"They'll be back," Mr. Simms said. "Let's go before I get mowed down."

With a little sigh, Chloe agreed, and they walked back to Sunnyview. Mr. Simms was quiet and didn't seem to want to talk anymore. And things had been going so well, Chloe thought.

As they entered Sunnyview, Lennon came through one of the hallways into the lobby. When he saw them, he stopped. "Did you guys go dancing?" he asked.

"Ha!" Simms snapped. "Went for a walk and found out the boardwalk's turned into a jungle. I almost got run over by a bunch of maniacs on roller skates!"

Lennon looked at Chloe. "Why didn't you say something?" he asked. "There's this skate club that practically takes over the boardwalk on Saturdays. I could have warned you."

Of course he could, she thought, gritting her teeth. After all, he knows everything!

chapter
five

"**M**anuelo, I need your advice," Chloe said. It was late Sunday morning. She was at the kitchen table, still in her short pink pajamas. Pepper lay next to her chair with her nose on Chloe's bare feet.

"Advice is my middle name," Manuelo said. He was at the counter, keeping an eye on the waffle iron. "What's the problem?"

Chloe sipped some orange juice. "Mr. Simms."

"Ah, your senior citizen."

"Right," Chloe said. "So here's my question: If you were a seventy-eight-year-old man, what would be your idea of fun?"

"Hmmm …" Manuelo tapped a finger on his chin. "I know! How about a sixty-five-year-old woman?"

"Manuelo, I'm serious!" Chloe said. "I really need ideas. So far I'm totally flunking in the hanging-with-the-seniors department."

"Let me think about it," Manuelo said. "In the meantime, eat some breakfast." He slid a waffle onto a plate and set it on the table.

Riley appeared in the doorway in her big yellow nightshirt. "Feed me!" she cried dramatically.

"Have a seat," Manuelo said, pouring more batter into the waffle iron. "Where's your mother?"

"In the shower." Riley got a glass from the cabinet. "I am totally starving. It must be all that shoveling we did yesterday."

"I thought you were going to be sawing wood," Chloe said, slipping a small bite of waffle to Pepper.

"Don't remind me." Riley groaned, opening the refrigerator. "The saw needs a new blade. And we couldn't have started on the benches anyway because the lumberyard isn't delivering the wood until tomorrow."

"But the flower beds are finished, right?" Chloe asked.

"Not yet," Riley said, pouring herself some orange juice and gulping it down. Then the phone rang and she grabbed it. "Hello?"

Chloe went back to nibbling her waffle. What else could she do with Mr. Simms? Maybe Riley could come up with something. Except Riley was so busy with the garden, Chloe didn't want to bother her.

Across the room, Riley suddenly gasped. "Larry did it?" she cried. "He asked you out?" She glanced at Chloe and pumped her fist in the air. "Sure we can go on a double date. Anything for the cause. I'll call Alex!"

Chloe gave her sister a thumbs-up. Larry asked Sierra out, she thought. Cool. Things were working out for Riley.

Now if they'd only work out for *her*.

"This is a disaster!" Riley cried at the garden the next afternoon. "Come on, Dean. You can't drop out *now*."

Dean sighed. "Sorry, Riley, but I have to. I never should have volunteered in the first place. My grades were kind of tanking before we even started, and I have to bring them up or I could get kicked off the team. Plus my parents will go ballistic if I fail anything."

"But…" Riley looked around. Shane and Larry were working in the flower beds. Lauren was washing the sculptures. Nobody was doing anything with the benches. "What about the benches?" she asked. "You said you'd help saw the new slats and put them in and everything."

"I know, but it's not rocket science," Dean told her. "And you can keep the saw as long as you need it."

"All right," Riley said. And Dean was right about one thing. Sawing wasn't rocket science. "Did you bring the new blade, at least?" she asked.

"Oops!" Dean said. "I'll bring it by tomorrow for sure." He turned and trotted away.

Do *not* worry, Riley told herself. You'll have the blade tomorrow. And how long can it take to saw some slats, anyway?

"Hey, there, Riley," George Watkins said, walking

around the corner of library. "Whoa," he added, glancing around. "I hate to say it, but I thought you'd be a little further along."

Riley cringed inside, but she made herself smile. "We're doing okay," she assured him. She pointed to Lauren, who was hosing off the sculptures. "The sculptures will be ready pretty soon. And we're going to finish the flower beds today."

"Uh-huh." George frowned a little. "What about the benches?"

Riley groaned to herself. Why did he have to ask? "The wood's been ordered," she said, deciding not to tell him exactly when it would be delivered.

George nodded. "I see you're missing two people today," he said.

"Well, Shane's visiting his grandparents," Riley explained. "And Dean..." She hesitated. She didn't want to tell him Dean had dropped out for good. "Dean had to leave," she said.

"Listen, Riley," George said. "I know you're working hard, but maybe I should step in. It's a big job for a fourteen-year-old to be the head of a team. And it doesn't look as if we're going to be ready by Saturday."

"We will!" Riley assured him. "I can handle this, Mr. Watkins. I have a real plan."

George gave her a doubtful look, but he finally nodded and left.

Take a deep breath, Riley told herself. Do not freak.

Freaking will not get the garden done. "Listen up, guys!" she called out. "Dean had to quit."

"Are you kidding me?" Lauren said.

"I wish," Riley told her. "Anyway, let's all work on the flower beds and finish getting them ready today, okay?"

"You're the boss," Larry said cheerfully.

"Right," Shane agreed.

"I'm sick of washing this stuff anyway," Lauren declared. She picked up another hoe and joined Riley in one of the flower beds.

Working hard and fast, the three of them unearthed rocks, turned up dirt, and spread out more of the topsoil.

Two hours later Riley was beginning to feel a little better. "We're doing it," she said. "We're really getting it done."

"That's because we have a great leader!" Larry replied.

"Thanks, Larry," she said. It was nice to have such loyal support. And even better, Larry wasn't hanging all over her or getting in the way today. Maybe he was thinking about Sierra. If so, that meant her plan was working. Thanks, Sierra, she thought.

An hour later it was time to go.

"See you tomorrow!" Lauren called as she left the garden.

Riley glanced around the garden. They still had so much to do. Fix the benches, put the bricks around the flower beds...

Oh, no! Riley thought. The flowers! I forgot to order them!

"Hey, look—here come Alex and Sierra," Larry said.

"Hi! Ready for some pizza?" Alex asked, slinging his arm around Riley's shoulders.

Riley snuggled close to him. She wanted to go, but how could she enjoy herself when she'd made such a big mistake?

"What's the matter?" Alex asked her.

Riley sighed and told him the problem. "How am I supposed to fix up a garden when I don't have any flowers?" she asked. "I mean, it's the most important thing! Maybe Mr. Watkins was right. Maybe I'm too young to handle such a big responsibility."

"No way," Alex said. "You can do it, Riley. I know you can."

"But there's so much to do!" Riley complained. "And I messed up big-time with the flowers."

"So call the flower store from the pizza place," Sierra suggested. "I'll help you plant them if you need me."

"Thanks, Sierra," Riley said. "I definitely need you."

"I just had a cool idea," Larry said. "Sierra could take Dean's place."

Sierra smiled at him. "That would be fun."

Larry slung an arm around Sierra's shoulders. "Major fun!"

"That's a great idea. Thanks, you guys." Riley gave Alex a kiss on the cheek. "Okay, let's get some pizza."

As they headed for Pizza Pizzazz, Riley started to relax. Larry didn't know it, but he'd come up with the perfect solution. Not only would Sierra help with the work, she'd help keep Larry busy.

Things were definitely looking up!

chapter six

"**I**'ve got it!" Manuelo said to Chloe as he passed through the living room late Monday afternoon. Mr. Simms had an appointment with the dentist, so she hadn't gone to Sunnyview. "Senior swim. The Y has swimming sessions just for senior citizens."

"Well…" Chloe said. At the moment, she was sitting on the couch, watching MTV and petting Pepper, who was sitting on her lap. "It's a good idea, but—"

"But what?" Manuelo sniffed. "It's an *excellent* idea."

"Definitely. It's excellent," Chloe agreed. "But I'm not sure he really wants to *do* anything. I need to find a way to talk to him again. We kind of started a cool conversation, but then these skaters messed everything up. And Mr. Simms got all grouchy again. And of course Lennon was there to see it, making me feel like an even bigger idiot."

"Ah." Manuelo swiped a dust rag across one of the

end tables. "Well, I'll try to think of some scintillating topics of conversation."

"Thanks, Manuelo," Chloe said as he left the room. The video ended, and Chloe switched channels. A fluffy, bright-eyed dog appeared on the screen. It trotted down a hallway and into a room full of elderly people. "The residents of the nursing home always look forward to Chester's visits," the narrator declared. "Holding him has a truly positive effect on their lives."

Chloe sat up straight, watching the little dog trot from person to person, nosing their hands and wagging his tail. Everybody was smiling.

That's it! Chloe thought. "Pepper, guess what?" she said to the puppy, who was now snoozing in her lap. "Tomorrow, you're coming with me to Sunnyview! If you can't soften up Mr. Simms, nobody can!"

Riley felt a little anxious as she hurried to the garden after school on Tuesday. The flower beds were ready, but they were also empty. She had ordered the flowers yesterday, but they wouldn't be delivered until later in the week. There were bricks to replace, and slats to cut and paint.

And only four days to do it all.

At least Dean remembered the new saw blade, she thought. He'd met her after school and given it to her. She rounded the corner of the library and almost bumped into George Watkins, her supervisor. "Hi, Mr. Watkins!"

"Hello, Riley. I was just checking things out again," he told her. "So what's on the agenda for this afternoon?" he asked.

Riley held up the saw blade in its cardboard sleeve. "New slats for the benches."

George nodded. "What about the flowers?"

"I'm on top of it," she assured him. She smiled. "Time to get to work!"

"Right. Oh, by the way," George added. "If you ordered mulch, you can cancel it. I did some planting at home and had ten bags left over. I just dropped it off."

"Ten bags—wow!" Riley exclaimed. "Thanks a lot. Bye!" She hurried around to where Larry, Lauren, and Shane were waiting for her. Sierra would come by right after orchestra practice. "Quick—somebody tell me what mulch is!" Riley demanded.

Lauren pointed to some bulging plastic bags stacked under a tree.

"Yeah, but what *is* it?" Riley asked.

"It's that stuff you put on the ground around bushes and trees," Larry said. "You know, little chips of wood."

"Oh, right!" Riley said. Who would ever guess that Larry would know the answer? "Okay, we don't have to do anything with it yet." She glanced around. "Let's finish the sculptures today," she said.

Lauren groaned, but went to work. Shane went with her. Larry followed Riley over to the saw. "Why don't I help you with the benches?" he said. "It'll go faster."

Riley watched in surprise as he removed the old blade and quickly put the new one in. Who would ever guess that Larry would know his way around a power saw?

"Hey, Riley, thanks for telling me to ask out Sierra," Larry said, tightening a screw. "She's really cool. She's even going out with me again. Awesome, huh?"

"Totally," Riley agreed. But she knew she would owe Sierra big for going out with Larry *twice*.

Larry held up the saw. "Done!"

This is so cool, Riley thought as she and Larry measured the slats together. Larry was obviously interested in Sierra, so he didn't bug Riley at all. And he was actually a big help!

Four more days. That's all I need. Just let this last for four more days!

"There's Sierra!" Larry cried as they measured the last slat. He handed the pencil to Riley and hurried over to Sierra.

Riley drew the line on the piece of wood and stuck the pencil in her pocket. She looked at Larry and Sierra. The two of them were talking together. Very close together. So close, their heads were touching.

Cute, Riley thought. Now they're holding hands. Now he's whispering in her ear, and she's laughing. Now they're walking away...wait a sec! Where are they going? There's work to do!

Riley started to call out, but then she saw Sierra lean even closer and kiss Larry on the cheek.

Whoa! she thought. Sierra doesn't just like him— she *likes* him!

Riley kept staring at Larry, trying to figure out what Sierra saw in him. His brown hair had turned a little blond from the sun. She couldn't see his eyes, but she knew they were brown. He *was* kind of cute, she guessed.

"Okay, Pepper, let's find Mr. Simms!" Chloe said as she led the puppy into Sunnyview that afternoon. "He's probably in the lounge. Come on!"

She couldn't wait for Mr. Simms's reaction. Pepper was so cute, Mr. Simms would have to smile. Then they'd start talking about dogs and pets and everything. This was really going to work!

Pepper wanted to sniff every square inch of the Sunnyview lobby, so Chloe finally picked her up. As she carried her toward the lounge, Lennon came through the front doors carrying a paint can. "Hey, a dog!" he said.

Chloe smiled. "This is Pepper," she told him. "I brought her to meet Mr. Simms."

Lennon scratched Pepper behind the ears. "She's pretty cute." He smiled at Chloe.

Chloe nodded. Wow, Lennon was being almost nice. "Mr. Simms is going to totally love her," she said. "I mean, who can resist?"

"Nobody," Lennon agreed. "Unless they're allergic to dogs. Or afraid of them."

Chloe groaned to herself. Great. With her luck, Mr. Simms would be both. But she wouldn't let Lennon have the satisfaction of knowing that. "Do you think I'd bring a dog to somebody who's allergic to them?" she asked.

"No way," Lennon said, patting the dog on the head. "Mr. Simms is going to love her."

Pepper started squirming in Chloe's arms. "Well, I should probably find Mr. Simms. See you later."

First, Chloe carried Pepper into the lounge. Amanda waved from the computer. Chloe waved back, but she didn't see Mr. Simms. She tried the sunroom next, but he wasn't there either. He must still be in his apartment, she decided. She went down the hall and rang his doorbell. "Mr. Simms?" she called, ringing the bell again.

"Hold your horses!" he called back. "I heard the bell. I'm not deaf, remember?"

"I remember, but wait!" Chloe said as the doorknob rattled. "Don't open the door yet. I have a question—are you allergic to dogs? Or scared of them?"

"That's two questions," he pointed out. "No to both of them. Why?"

"Open the door and you'll see!" Chloe told him.

The doorknob rattled again. Then the door opened, and Mr. Simms's frowning face appeared.

"Mr. Simms, meet Pepper!" Chloe said proudly. "Pepper, say hi to Mr. Simms!" She hoisted the dog up a little higher and waved Pepper's paw at him.

"Pepper?" Mr. Simms reached out and stroked the dog's head. "Cute name. Cute dog."

Pepper licked his hand and squirmed harder. "She likes you," Chloe said. "Scratch her behind the ears, she loves that."

"Most dogs do," he agreed, giving the dog a scratch. "Hey, Pepper," he said. "How are you doing?"

Was I right or what? Chloe thought. Mr. Simms is totally melting! "Is it okay if I put her down?" she asked. "She's really wiggling."

"Sure." Mr. Simms stepped back, and Chloe set Pepper on the floor. With an excited bark, Pepper shot through the door and sniffed his shoes. "Hey, puppy!" he said, laughing.

Pepper circled his legs and barked again.

This is so cool! Chloe thought—until Pepper squatted and peed right on the foyer rug.

chapter
seven

"**O**h, no! Pepper!" Chloe gasped. "Mr. Simms, I'm so sorry!"

Mr. Simms stared at the wet spot on the rug.

"I'm so sorry!" she repeated. She picked up Pepper and backed out of the doorway. "Let me find someplace to put her and I'll come right back and clean it!"

Mr. Simms shook his head. "Don't bother. I can—"

"No. I'll do it," Chloe protested. "This is totally my fault. Pepper's housebroken—really—but she was excited and nervous, I guess. Anyway, I'll be right back!"

She scurried down the hallway with Pepper wiggling in her arms. "Don't worry, I still love you," she murmured as the dog licked her chin. "But what a mess!"

When Chloe reached the lobby, Lennon was coming through the front doors again, this time with rollers and a paint tray. "Is there someplace I can leave Pepper?" she asked, hoping he wouldn't ask what happened.

"How come you want to leave her somewhere?" Lennon asked. "I thought—"

"She messed up Mr. Simms's rug and I need to go clean it up," Chloe blurted out. Then she braced herself. Here comes a smart remark, she thought.

But Lennon surprised her. "I could take her out front and tie her leash to one of those planters," he offered, putting his painting stuff down. He smiled at the dog. "Hey, Pepper, wanna go outside?"

"That would be great, thanks!" She set Pepper on the floor and sped back to Mr. Simms's apartment.

The door was still open. Chloe found Mr. Simms jabbing his cane at some paper towels he'd draped over the wet spot.

"I'll do that," Chloe said.

Mr. Simms moved aside, and Chloe knelt down. The towels were soaked and shredded. She dumped them in a small wastebasket and glanced around.

A whole roll of towels sat on the foyer table. As Chloe reached for it, she noticed the dozens of framed photographs on the wall above the table. Some were in black and white, some in color. All of them showed people dancing or mingling at parties, laughing and having a great time.

Chloe ripped off more towels and started blotting the stain. So Mr. Simms really did used to be a party animal, she thought. She wondered who all the people were, but maybe this wasn't the best time to ask him.

Mr. Simms cleared his throat. "How's it coming?"

"Done," Chloe told him. "Tomorrow I'll bring some special stuff to disinfect the rug. We used it when we were training Pepper. Believe me, it works."

Chloe tossed the towels in the wastebasket and stood up. "I'm going to check on Pepper, but I'll be right back, okay?"

"Tomorrow's better," Mr. Simms said, ushering Chloe into the hall. "Right now, I feel a snooze coming on. Uh, thanks for the cleanup." He shut the door.

At least he didn't *slam* the door, Chloe thought. But she had the definite feeling that Mr. Simms wasn't sleepy at all. He just wanted to get rid of her.

With a sigh, Chloe went back to the lobby. She opened the front door and found Lennon setting a bowl of water down next to Pepper. "Hi," he said when Chloe came out. "I thought she might get thirsty."

[Chloe: He's still being nice. This is weird. Will the real Lennon Porter please stand up?]

"Thanks," Chloe said as Pepper lapped up the water.

"No problem. Just don't let her near Mr. Simms's rug for a while." He looked around. "Where *is* Mr. Simms, anyway?"

"He wanted to take a nap."

"Really?" Lennon grinned. "Well, like I said, you really know how to liven up somebody's day!"

[Chloe: Okay, Lennon, you can sit down now.]

• • •

Ignoring Chloe and Manuelo, Riley stomped into the kitchen later that afternoon and yanked open the refrigerator door. "Are we out of root beer?" she asked grumpily.

"No," Manuelo replied, chopping up some celery.

"I don't see it," Riley declared.

"Perhaps because we have never had any root beer in the first place," Manuelo explained. "So how can we be out of it?"

Riley shrugged. She wasn't in the mood for jokes. She started shoving cans and bottles around, looking for something else to drink.

"I was just telling Manuelo about my latest disaster with Mr. Simms," Chloe said, propping her elbows on the kitchen table.

"Ha. You want to hear about a disaster?" Riley grabbed a bottle and slammed the refrigerator door. "Wait till I tell you what happened at the garden!"

"Okay, but, Riley?" Chloe said.

"What?"

"You don't really want to drink soy sauce, do you?" Chloe asked.

Riley looked at the bottle. LOW-SODIUM SOY SAUCE.

Manuelo held his hand out. "I'll take it. I'm making a stir-fry for dinner."

Riley gave him the bottle and flopped into a chair. "I am so mad!" she declared.

"No kidding," Chloe said. "What happened?"

"Larry and Sierra disappeared on me, can you believe it?" Riley said. "I mean, we've only got four—no, now it's three—days left to finish the garden, and there's a ton of stuff to do."

"Whoa—go back," Chloe said. "They disappeared?"

"Well, not for good," Riley grumbled. "See, when Sierra showed up to work, Larry practically started drooling. Actually, they both did. Then they started talking and holding hands and everything...."

Chloe grinned. "Really? Cool!"

Riley frowned. "Not cool. I thought they were going to hang for just a few minutes, but they actually left! I needed help with the benches, so I had to find Larry and it took forever. Guess where they were?"

"Were they sitting in a tree? K-I-S-S-I-N-G?" Manuelo asked.

"No," Riley said. "They were checking out the new computers in the library."

Chloe sighed. "Ah. Romance!"

"This isn't funny," Riley told her. "When we got back to the garden, Lauren and Shane were gone. They both have big tests tomorrow. At least *they* left me a note! And Mr. Watkins was there again. He wanted to know where everybody was and why we weren't working!"

"And did you explain?" Manuelo asked.

"I tried, but I could tell he thought I was just making excuses." Riley huffed out a big breath. "I still can't believe Larry went off like that. And Sierra! She knows how stressed I am about this project, but she just dragged him away!"

"Well, but Riley, you can't be mad at them," Chloe said. "Don't you remember what it was like when you and Alex first got together? You wanted to be with each other every second."

"Yeah, but Sierra was supposed to go out with Larry so he'd stop bugging me," Riley argued. "This wasn't supposed to turn into a major romance."

"Shh. What's that?" Manuelo put a hand to his ear. "Riley, is that jealousy I hear?"

"Me? Jealous?" Riley laughed. "Get real! I mean, jealous of what?"

chapter
eight

After a hot shower and some of Manuelo's chicken stir-fry, Riley felt much calmer. Jealous, she thought. Manuelo just made a big deal out of nothing. All I needed was a good gripe session.

She logged on to the Internet. She was supposed to do some research for a history paper, but first things first—she checked her Buddy List. Sierra was on-line.

    RILEY241: Hi, Sierra, it's me. What R U
    doing?

    SIERRA-LALA: Hanging. R U still mad at
    Larry and me?

    RILEY241: No. Forget it.

Just don't go wandering off anymore, she thought.

SIERRA-LALA: OK. Wait. Back in a sec.

Riley checked her list and saw that Larry was on-line now. Was Sierra talking to him? She waited. A few seconds later Sierra came back.

SIERRA-LALA: Guess what? Larry found my silver bracelet! I noticed it was missing when we were walking home. I thought it was gone 4-ever, but he walked back every step and found it!

RILEY241: Cool.

Riley clicked on Larry's name.

RILEY241: Hi, Larry.

LARRYXLNT: Hi, Riley. Sierra says you're not mad anymore. :) We didn't mean to skip out on you.

RILEY241: Okay. Listen, what do U think about the garden? Mr. Watkins is nervous, but we can get it done if we work really hard. Right?

Riley waited, but Larry didn't reply. Sierra didn't come back either. Riley stared at her screen and waited some more. Had they forgotten about her or something? Finally, Sierra came back.

```
SIERRA-LALA: Hi! Larry just told me a
super-funny joke! I'm still laughing!

RILEY241: Tell me! Tell me!
```

Riley kept waiting, but her screen stayed blank. She scowled at it. What was with them, anyway? How could they just ignore her like this? She liked Larry's jokes, too.

```
RILEY241: Hey, Larry, tell me the joke.
I could use some yucks. :)

LARRYXLNT: Tell U tomorrow. Sierra and I
are planning something. Bye 4 now.
```

Did Larry just do what I think he did? Did he just dump me on-line? Well, he *is* interested in Sierra now, Riley reminded herself. Just like I wanted, right?

Riley slumped down her chair, feeling angry and left out and…and what? What was going on with her?

"Okay, hold it steady, Riley," Larry said the next day at the garden. He pulled on a pair of clear plastic goggles.

Hey, his eyes aren't solid brown, Riley thought, tightening her grip on the wooden slat. There's a little green around the middle. How come I never noticed that before?

"Uh, Riley?" Larry said.

She blinked. "Huh?"

Larry pointed to the slat. "Your hands are in the way."

"Oh!" Riley quickly moved her hands away from the pencil line. Was I actually checking Larry out? she wondered. She *was*. And she had to admit, for some weird reason he looked cute today!

"Ready?" Larry asked.

Riley tightened her grip. "Go!"

Larry thumbed the switch on the power saw and zipped it through the wood. "That's one!" he shouted over the saw's loud whine.

Riley put the cut slat aside and picked up the second one. She set it across the sawhorses.

Larry's face broke into a huge smile.

[**Riley**: Okay, I knew this couldn't last forever. Here it comes. Watch this. He's going to ask me out again.]

"Sierra! Over here!" Larry cried.

Riley turned to see Sierra crossing the garden toward them.

"I brought your bracelet with me," Larry said when she reached them. He patted his pocket.

"Great! Keep it there for now, okay?" Sierra kissed his cheek.

Riley tensed up. The last thing she wanted to do

was watch Sierra kiss Larry. Sure, getting Sierra and Larry together was all her idea. But it was supposed to be temporary—only until the garden was finished. She never imagined that Sierra would actually *like* Larry.

And what made it even worse was that Riley was beginning to think that she had made a mistake. All these years and she'd never given Larry a real chance. Maybe she should have.

"I'm ready to work, Riley," Sierra said. "What do you want me to do?"

Larry put his arm around Sierra's shoulders. "Want to help me finish cutting these slats?"

"Sure!" Sierra agreed. "But only if I get to wear some of those cute plastic goggles."

Larry grinned and handed her a pair.

"Hey, Riley!" Shane shouted from across the garden. He pointed to the marble bench top. "How do we clean this?"

Let me out of here, Riley thought as she headed over to Shane. She glanced over her shoulder and saw Larry help Sierra untangle her hair from the goggle strap. They were both giggling.

I should have realized this was going to happen. Larry's not going to work as hard with Sierra around. Why did Sierra have to join the group? And how could Larry fall for her so fast, anyway? I mean, they went on one stupid date.

Stop it! Riley told herself. This was your idea,

remember? You can't be jealous. You just can't be!

Riley and Shane washed and polished the marble, then helped Lauren work on the rest of the sculptures for an hour. They spent time setting some of the bricks around the flower beds, but the new ones hadn't arrived yet, so they couldn't finish.

Soon Shane and Lauren had to leave.

Riley walked over to Larry and Sierra, who were drilling holes into the slats.

Sierra turned off the drill. "That's the last one, Riley. Are Larry and I a great team, or what?" She held out her hand.

Larry slapped Sierra's palm, then curled his fingers through hers. "Let's put the stuff away and then we're outta here."

"Wait—you're leaving?" Riley asked.

"We both have tests tomorrow, so we're studying together," Sierra explained.

Yeah, right. They're going to spend half the time kissing, Riley thought. She could hardly stand to picture it! "Can't you study later?" she asked.

Sierra shook her head. "You know my mother makes me practice the violin for an hour every day. By the time I finish, it'll be too late for Larry to come over."

"Oh. Well, could you stay just a little longer?" Riley pointed to the slats. "At least long enough to sand those so we can paint them tomorrow?"

Larry looked at Sierra. "It's fine with me," he said,

squeezing her hand. "What about you? Is it okay?"

"Sure. For a little while," she agreed.

"Thanks." Riley took some sandpaper from one of the toolboxes and handed it out. Riley tried not to watch as Larry and Sierra worked together. But she couldn't stop sneaking glances at them. Especially at Larry.

His hair wasn't as spiky as it used to be. He must have let it grow. When did that happen? And why didn't I notice?

His smile didn't look so goofy, either. It was crooked, but actually kind of sweet.

Still watching Larry, Riley accidentally sanded her thumb. "Owwww!" It really hurt. She glanced at Larry again. Why wasn't he running over to make sure she was okay?

And why do I care? she wondered. But deep down, she knew the answer. She was starting to like Larry. *Really* like him.

About an hour later, Riley walked into her bedroom. I finally have a crush on Larry and now it's too late! She couldn't believe it.

Chloe was on her bed listening to Sheryl Crow. As soon as she saw Riley, she turned down the volume. "Mr. Simms didn't show up today," she announced. "I was going to finish cleaning his rug, remember?"

Riley barely heard her. Why didn't I ever notice that Larry was cute and funny before? she wondered. Why didn't I at least give him a real chance?

"But Mrs. Carpenter told me he had another appointment with the dentist," Chloe went on. "That's what *he* told *her*, anyway."

"Mmm," Riley murmured, changing her sweatshirt. Sierra always said she thought Larry was sweet. *Why didn't I listen to her?*

"That's two dentist appointments in one week, though," Chloe said. "Very suspicious. I bet he didn't want to see me. He's probably going to fire me. Can you even fire a volunteer?"

"Mmm," Riley mumbled again. She took off her jeans and put on a pair of pajama bottoms.

"If Lennon finds out Mr. Simms doesn't want to hang out with me anymore, he'll never stop laughing," Chloe said. "What do you think I should do?"

"Uh…" Riley sat on the edge of her bed. "Huh?"

Chloe frowned at her. "Did you hear one word of what I just said?"

"Sure. Mr. Simms didn't show up today," Riley replied. "And…um…give me a hint."

"You're obviously in another zone," Chloe said. "What are you thinking about?"

"Nothing," Riley said quickly. "I mean, nothing but the garden." *And Larry,* she added silently.

But Riley could never tell Chloe that she liked their goofy next-door neighbor. Chloe probably wouldn't believe her if she did. No, Riley couldn't tell anybody. This crush had to be a total and complete secret.

chapter
nine

"Riley, you're not listening again," Chloe said the next afternoon.

"I am, too," Riley replied, which was kind of a lie, but not a total one. She was half listening. Maybe a third. But the rest of her thoughts were on Larry. School was over, and she was on her way to the library garden. Chloe was walking over with her, then going on to the retirement home. "You were talking about Lennon Porter," she added.

And Larry actually has muscles in his arms, she thought. She'd noticed them yesterday when he was running the power saw. Another thing she'd never seen before because she'd never bothered to really look at him.

"Riley," Chloe said. "I stopped talking about Lennon a block and a half ago."

"Oh," Riley said. "Sorry. I'm just worrying about the garden," she explained. Larry and Sierra would be there, too, and she'd have to watch them fool around. It was going to be awful.

Riley sighed and glanced around. Down the block, she spotted a house with long tables on the front lawn. "Look, a yard sale," she said. "Let's check it out."

"I thought you were in a hurry," Chloe said.

"I am, but what's five minutes?" Riley argued. It'll be five minutes less of seeing Larry flirt with Sierra, she thought. "Maybe we'll find some clothes so old, they're cool again."

Riley began poking through a pile of tops on one of the tables. They were old, but not cool. Just out of style.

"Riley, look what I found!" Chloe cried. She held up a tarnished silver frame with a black-and-white photograph behind cracked glass. A group of dressed-up people sat around a table, raising their drinks to one another in a toast.

Chloe rubbed some dust from the bottom right corner. "See what it says there?"

Riley peered at it. "'Simms Photography.'"

Chloe nodded. "Mr. Simms told me he used to take pictures. I bet he'll get a laugh out of seeing this one with his name on it." She paused. "Riley, you're in another zone again. Or is it the same one? Anyway, what is up with you?"

Should I tell her? Riley wondered. No. It's way too embarrassing. "Nothing's up," she insisted. She looked at her watch. "Yikes! Gotta go, Chloe. See you later!"

I have got to get it together, Riley thought as she hurried to the garden.

Larry, Sierra, and Lauren were already there when Riley arrived. The first thing Riley noticed was that Larry and Sierra were holding hands.

"Hi," Riley said. "Where's Shane?"

"He said to tell you he'd be a little late," Larry replied. "Sierra and I are going to paint the slats, okay?"

Not okay, Riley thought. She wanted Larry to work with *her*. But he's not into me anymore, she reminded herself. He's interested in Sierra. "Sure," she said.

Larry and Sierra got busy stirring some dark green paint. The new bricks had arrived, and Riley and Lauren began setting them around the flower-bed borders.

Shane showed up a little while later and helped them.

Riley tried to concentrate. She managed not to look at Larry and Sierra very often, but she couldn't help hearing them. Larry would say something, Sierra would laugh, and Riley would feel left out. Larry used to try to make *her* laugh all the time.

When Sierra broke into another loud laugh, Riley finally glanced over. "Hey, could you guys stop kidding around?" she called out. "I mean, it's not like we have forever to finish!"

"We're just talking," Sierra said, giving Riley a funny look.

"Sorry," she said, feeling bad for snapping. Why was she taking this out on Sierra? It wasn't her fault.

Larry put his arm around Sierra's shoulders. "Let's whisper from now on," he said.

Sierra giggled, and the two of them went back to work.

"Okay, Riley, I'm going now," Shane said.

"Now? Didn't you just get here?" Riley exclaimed.

"Actually, I got here an hour ago," Shane told her. "But anyway, I'll see you tomorrow."

As Shane took off, Riley glanced around. Lauren was hosing off her hands. She was obviously leaving, too. Most of the bricks were in place, but something was missing.

The flowers! Riley thought. The garden store told me to call back and double-check about when to send them and I forgot!

Waving good-bye to Lauren, Riley hurried over to the shade tree where she'd left her backpack. She took out her cell phone and punched in the number of the garden store. Busy. She waited a few seconds, then hit redial. Still busy.

While Riley was waiting to try again, Larry and Sierra strolled over and picked up their backpacks.

Riley snapped the phone closed. "What's going on? You're not leaving, too, are you?"

Larry nodded. "We're done with the slats. The first coat, anyway. We can't give them a second one until tomorrow."

"Right, they're still wet," Sierra said.

"Okay, but why are you going?" Riley asked. "There's

still work to do. I wanted to start putting the mulch around."

"But we have plans," Sierra said. "Besides, don't you have to wait until you plant the flowers?"

Riley frowned. Okay, so Sierra's right, she thought. Does she have to make me sound stupid? She looked around. "Yes, but we can put it around the bushes," she said. "And the bags are really heavy. I could use some help lifting them. Maybe your plans can wait until later."

Larry squeezed Sierra's hand. "Come on. Riley needs us," he said.

"Okay," Sierra agreed. She frowned at Riley. "I guess we can stay a *little* while longer."

Riley suddenly felt guilty. She knew that she was making them stay to delay their date. But Riley couldn't help it. Why should Sierra have Larry all to herself?

When Chloe arrived at Sunnyview, she took a quick scan of the lobby. Lennon was nowhere in sight. Good. If he saw her, she knew he'd make some remark about Mr. Simms and the dentist.

Now to find Mr. Simms. If he wasn't going to stand her up again, he'd probably be in the lounge. She walked across the lobby.

"Chloe Carlson!" Lennon called out from behind her.

Chloe rolled her eyes and turned around. Lennon had just come through the door. "Hi," she said.

"Having trouble finding Mr. Simms?" he asked with a grin. "You could always check with his dentist."

"Very funny," Chloe said. "For your information, I am not having trouble finding him."

"Oh? Then why are you going into the lounge?"

"Because...what do you mean?" Chloe demanded.

Lennon smiled. "It's just that I saw him going into the sunroom about ten minutes ago."

At least he's *here*, Chloe thought, relieved. She swept past Lennon into the sunroom. Mr. Simms lay on a recliner with a newspaper over his stomach, snoring.

Chloe hesitated. Mr. Simms obviously didn't care whether she showed up or not. He probably hoped she *wouldn't*. Maybe she should just go home.

But she really wanted to try one more time. She didn't know why Mr. Simms was so grumpy. Maybe he was lonely or something. She knew there was a warm side to him, too. Their talk on the boardwalk proved that.

Mr. Simms snorted and jerked in his sleep. The newspaper slid to the floor with a loud rustle. Then his eyes snapped open and he stared at Chloe.

Chloe smiled and gave him a little wave. "How are you today, Mr. Simms?" she said with a smile.

"Huh...oh." He sat up slowly, swinging his legs over the side of the recliner. "Hello, Miss...uh...Chloe."

"Hi!" Chloe said. "I brought the stuff to clean your rug. It's in my backpack. And I found something I want to show you."

Chloe grabbed a chair and dragged it over to the recliner. She unzipped her backpack and took out the photograph she'd found at the yard sale. "Look," she said, pointing to the 'Simms Photography' at the bottom. "I found it at a yard sale. I mean, I know it's a coincidence, but I couldn't resist getting it, since it has your name on it."

Simms took the picture and gazed at it. He squinted at the frame. Then he smiled.

Chloe couldn't help smiling, too.

"It's not a coincidence," Simms said. "I took this picture."

"No way! You did?" Chloe asked.

Simms nodded. "I had my own photography studio. It was pretty successful, too. People came to me whenever they wanted a portrait—babies, engagements, the whole family."

"That is so cool," Chloe said. "This isn't a portrait, though. You must have done weddings and parties and things."

"Yep, I liked that the best—taking candid shots," Simms said. "I liked the parties. There was always music and food." He smiled again. "And pretty ladies."

Chloe laughed. "Yeah, you've got a reputation, you know."

Mr. Simms chuckled.

"Hey, was that a laugh?" Chloe asked.

"I believe it was." Mr. Simms glanced at her. "And is

it my imagination, or have you finally stopped chirping at me like a bird?"

Whoa! Chloe thought. I didn't even know I had stopped using my "happy voice." "I guess so," she said.

"Good. I like it better," Simms told her. "Your 'old folks' voice drove me crazy."

"I'm sorry," Chloe said. "I promise never to use it again if you promise never to be grouchy again. Or is that even possible?" she teased.

"We'll see." He chuckled.

Chloe grinned. They were actually talking and joking. This was awesome!

Mr. Simms tapped the photograph. "I remember this one. It was a family reunion. In 1961, I think."

Chloe had an idea. "Hey, the yard sale's just a few blocks away. Why don't we go there? Maybe the people will remember you."

"I doubt it. It was a long time ago," Mr. Simms said. "But...I like yard sales."

"You do?" Chloe jumped up. "Then why didn't you say so?"

"You never asked," Mr. Simms shot back.

Chloe rolled her eyes. Then she laughed and held out her hand. "Come on, Mr. Simms. Let's go!"

chapter
ten

"**B**usy again?" Riley cried, snapping her phone shut in frustration. "It must be the most popular garden center on the planet!"

She gazed around the garden. Larry and Sierra had just left, so Riley was alone.

[**Riley**: And I'm talking to myself. A definite sign that I'm losing it.]

"Hi, there, Riley!" George Watkins said, walking around the corner of the library. "Only two days to go!"

Riley groaned silently. Only *two*? Would it ever be done? "Right!" she exclaimed, hoping she sounded confident and enthusiastic. "It's going to be great, too. Look, we put out a lot of the mulch already, and painted the slats for the benches."

"They look good." George strolled over to the slats of wood, which were lying across some sawhorses.

"We'll give them a second coat tomorrow," Riley added.

He nodded. "What kind of varnish are you going to use?"

[Riley: Varnish? Is he kidding?]

"They'll need it, you know," George said. "Otherwise, the paint job won't last."

[Riley: He's not kidding.]

"Definitely," Riley agreed. Note to self, she thought: Buy varnish.

"And the varnish will take time to dry." George scanned the garden. "Well, the bushes look great. And I never thought you'd get those sculptures cleaned, but you did it."

"Thanks!" Riley said.

A small frown appeared on George's face. "When will the flowers be here?" he asked.

Riley groaned to herself again. Why hadn't she called the garden center earlier? "Soon," she told him.

George's frown deepened.

"Please don't worry, Mr. Watkins," she told him. "Everything will be done in time for Saturday's big opening, I promise!"

"I hope so, Riley," he said. "We have a lot of people coming to the opening."

After he left, Riley took a deep breath. She'd

promised to get everything finished, but was it really possible?

It has to be, she thought. I've already messed up my chances with Larry. I can't mess this up, too!

Feeling totally stressed, she checked the bench slats, but they were still wet. I need time! she thought. I need help! I need—flowers!

She dialed the flower center one more time. At last, her call went through. Unfortunately, she got a recording telling her the store was closed for the day.

Riley sighed. She was stuck—there was nothing else she could do until tomorrow. She stored the tools in the library's basement and headed home. She passed by Pizza Pizzazz and caught a whiff of tomatoes and cheese. Her stomach growled. She started to go in, then stopped.

Larry and Sierra were sitting at a table by the window. They were holding hands and smiling at each other.

Should she go inside? She'd definitely be butting in. And did she really want to sit and watch Larry holding Sierra's hand?

No, but she was hungry, too. She should be able to go into a pizza place if she wanted to. She decided she would eat really fast and then leave.

Riley pushed open the door and walked over to their table. "Hi, you guys, can I join you?"

Sierra gave her a look that said "No."

"Sure, sit down, Riley," Larry said.

Riley pulled a chair up to the table. "I'm totally wiped out," she said, leaning her head back and closing her eyes. "And starving."

"I was about to get Sierra another Coke. Want me to get you a slice of pizza?" Larry offered.

"Thanks, Larry, that would be great."

"Be right back." Larry stood up and went to the counter.

Sierra just stared at her.

Riley had no idea what to say. "So, um, what's up?"

"I don't get it, Riley. What are you doing?" Sierra said.

"What do you mean?" Riley asked, opening her eyes wide, even though she knew exactly what Sierra was talking about.

"Well, it's just that Larry and I were hanging out and you kind of, you know, barged in. Didn't you see the way I looked at you?" Sierra asked. "I didn't want you to sit down."

Riley straightened up. She knew she shouldn't feel insulted, but she did. So, now that Sierra and Larry were a couple, Riley wasn't allowed to hang out with them?

"I guess I was just too tired to catch the signal," Riley said. "You know I've been working like crazy. And listen, I would appreciate it if you wouldn't hog Larry for a day or so, or this project might not get finished."

"Hog *Larry*?" Sierra cried. Her eyes flashed angrily. "That's what you wanted, Riley! First you beg me to go out with him, and now that we're having fun, you suddenly change your mind?"

Riley wanted to say yes, but she just couldn't tell Sierra the truth. This had to be the worst day of her life.

She was messing up the garden project *and* hurting her friendship with Sierra!

chapter eleven

Riley's in her zone again, Chloe thought Thursday night. The two of them were sitting at the kitchen table after dinner. Manuelo was at the counter, making a shopping list.

Chloe gazed at her sister, who was writing in a notebook. "Riley, is something wrong?" she asked.

Riley glanced up. "Huh?"

"You're so quiet," Chloe said. "I know you're busy, but you've been acting weird lately."

"It's the garden," Riley replied. "We only have a day left to finish it, and I'm really stressed."

Hmm. Chloe wondered if that was the whole story. But what else could it be? She sneaked a peek at Riley's notebook. Reading upside down was tricky, but she managed a few words. *Finish mulch*! *Flowers*!! *Varnish*!!!

[<u>Chloe</u>: Whoa—look at all those exclamation points. Maybe the only problem really is the garden.]

"You'll never guess what I found out about Mr. Simms," Chloe said, changing the subject. "The bulletin board at Sunnyview has a list of everybody's birthday, and Mr. Simms's birthday is Saturday!"

"Uh-huh," Riley murmured.

"I'm going to throw him a surprise party," Chloe declared. "I asked Mrs. Carpenter, and she thought it was a great idea. So I'm going to make invitations on the computer and put them in everybody's mailbox at the retirement home."

"Very nice," Manuelo said.

Riley closed her notebook. "Yeah, except I thought you and Mr. Simms didn't get along."

"We do now," Chloe told her. "The whole thing was my fault. I was so busy trying to prove to Lennon that I was good at hanging with senior citizens, I didn't realize how fake I was being. Mr. Simms saw right through it. Anyway, I can't wait to have the party for him."

Manuelo glanced up from his list. "Shall I pick up the ingredients for a cake tomorrow? And bake it?"

Chloe grinned. Her cooking skills were practically zilch. "Thanks, Manuelo. I was sort of hoping you'd say that. Amanda said she'd bring paper plates, and Quinn's bringing soda. I'll take care of the balloons and decorations. But I want to do something more."

"Like what?" Riley asked.

Chloe shook her head. "I don't know. I just want it to be spectacular."

"Did somebody say spectacular?" Macy asked, walking into the kitchen. "Look at this!" She held out her arm, and Tedi strode in wearing a slinky red dress with a plunging neckline and matching six-inch heels.

Manuelo whistled.

"Wow, Mom, is that your latest creation?" Chloe asked.

Macy nodded as Tedi strutted around the room, striking poses. "What do you think?"

"It's gorgeous," Chloe declared. "Totally."

Manuelo whistled again. "Tedi, you are one foxy lady!"

Suddenly Chloe got the most amazing idea. It was perfect for Mr. Simms's party. And it was going to be spectacular!

"Riley, is everything okay?" Alex asked in school the next day. "You're kind of quiet."

"Me?" Riley asked. First Chloe and now Alex, she thought. I have to do a better job of acting normal. "I'm great," she said. "Just a little worried about the garden." And I have a crush on Larry, she thought. I'm walking down the hall, holding Alex's hand, and thinking about Larry. Otherwise, no problem!

Alex squeezed her hand. "You'll get it finished, don't worry. I wish I could come help, but I've got a major paper to write, and my dad wants me to help clean out the garage and—"

"It's okay," Riley said. Having Alex at the garden might make things even more complicated, she thought.

Alex squeezed her hand again, then pointed down the hallway. "There's Sierra. Come on, I need to ask her something. Hey, Sierra, hang on a sec!"

Sierra peered out from behind her locker door. "Hi, Alex." She paused. "Hi, Riley," she said coolly.

"Hi." Riley smiled, but Sierra didn't smile back.

She's still angry, Riley thought, listening to the two of them discuss a song the band was working on. And I don't blame her!

The bell rang. Alex gave Riley a quick kiss, then went to his first class. Sierra slammed her locker. She and Riley had the same first-period class. If things were normal, they'd be walking together. But Sierra hurried off by herself.

Things are definitely not normal, Riley thought. Feeling miserable, she followed Sierra down the hall to sewing class. Larry was already there.

Riley's heart sank. Larry had had a crush on her for years. But now that she had a crush on *him*, she couldn't ask him out or even tell him she was interested, not when Sierra liked him.

Riley's desk was between Larry's and Sierra's. When she sat down, Larry gave her a quick smile. Sierra glared at her.

I so totally blew it! Riley thought.

"Good morning, class." Ms. Spoke, the sewing teacher, walked into the room. "Let's see…your projects are due next week, so you know what to do!"

Riley got her half-done pillow cover from a shelf by

the window and sat back down. Larry started working on his and talking to Sierra, too. Riley felt totally in the way.

After a minute, Riley stopped threading her machine and glanced at Larry as he ripped out some crooked stitching. His hands were tan, with long, slender fingers. Riley wondered what it would be like to hold one of those hands.

She stared at her pillow cover, but in her mind she was imagining a scene with Larry. They're walking on the beach, holding hands. Then Larry lets go and puts his arm around her waist. She snuggles against him. The sunset is spectacular, and they stop to watch it. She looks at him. He looks at her and smiles. He pulls her against him. His lips get closer and closer.

[Riley: Cut! Something's wrong with this scene. But what?]

Riley tried again. This time, she pictured the two of them at a movie. Larry puts his arm around her. She could feel him watching her. She glances at him. He smiles. His lips get closer and closer....

[Riley: No, no, no! It's still not right!]

Riley tried a third time, but it still didn't work. It was totally impossible to imagine kissing Larry. But why? After all, she had a crush on him, right? So why couldn't she picture kissing him? What was the problem?

chapter
twelve

"**Y**ou're a lifesaver, Dad!" Riley exclaimed as her father dropped her off at the library on Friday afternoon. "Thanks for taking me to the hardware store."

"No problem, honey," Jake said. He handed Riley a can of varnish and the brushes they'd bought. "If you need anything else, just let me know."

Riley thanked him again and hurried around back to the garden. Shane, Larry, and Lauren were just putting their backpacks under the tree. "Hi, everybody!" she called. "It's crunch time—tomorrow's the grand opening, so we have to finish today."

"Today?" Lauren looked around doubtfully. "Oh, boy."

"We can do it!" Larry declared. "What's first, Riley?"

"First...wait," Riley said. "Where's Sierra?"

"She couldn't come," Larry replied. "I don't know why exactly. She just said to tell you she couldn't make it."

Riley felt herself blushing with guilt. I know exactly

why, she thought. Sierra's so angry, she doesn't even want to be around me!

But Riley couldn't think about it now. There wasn't time. Not with everything that had to be done. "Okay!" she said, clapping her hands together. "Here's the plan. Larry and Shane, you guys put that marble bench back together. Then put a second coat of paint on the slats. Lauren and I will start planting the flowers."

"What flowers?" Shane asked.

"Huh?" Riley looked around. "Oh, no! Where *are* they?"

"Want me to get them, Riley?" Larry asked.

"Uh…no, thanks," she said. Larry obviously didn't have a clue how many flowers they were talking about. "You and Shane do the marble bench," she told him. "I'll call the store again."

"You're the boss," Larry agreed with a grin. "Come on, Shane. It's muscle time!"

"I'll put some mulch down around the sculptures," Lauren said as Riley punched the garden center's number on her cell phone. "I think it'll look good, don't you?"

"Great, thanks." We can still do this, Riley thought, listening to the phone ring. Can't we?

The man at the garden center wasn't the same one Riley had talked to before. "But he told me he'd have the flowers delivered!" Riley said. "I really, really need them. Like now!"

The man finally agreed to send the flowers. Riley

thanked him a zillion times. She shut her phone, and Larry and Shane ran up to her.

"Mission accomplished!" Larry reported. He snapped a salute and accidentally poked himself in the eye.

Riley shook her head at him. "Don't try that again, Larry. I need you to be able to see."

"Right," Larry agreed, blinking. "Okay. What's next?"

"Shane, you help Lauren," Riley directed. "Larry, let's paint." At least Larry and I will get to spend some time together, Riley thought. Just like old times.

[Riley: Okay, just like a week ago, but who's counting?]

Larry followed Riley to the sawhorses. He reached down for the can of paint and knocked off three of the wooden slats.

Riley gasped.

"Don't worry, they're okay," Larry said, grabbing the slats off the ground. "See? Not a scratch!"

"But are they dry?" Riley asked.

Larry ran his hand down one of them. "Dry as a bone!" He laid them across the sawhorses and reached for the paint again. Two more slats fell.

Riley rolled her eyes. "Oh, Larry..."

[Riley: Wait. Did I just roll my eyes at him? I did! But you don't do that to a boy you have a crush on, do you?]

Larry began prying the lid off a paint can with a screwdriver. "It's kind of stuck," he muttered.

"Careful, don't ..." Riley gasped again as the lid flipped off and hit her in the knee. "...pop it," she finished, looking at the smear of dark green paint on her jeans. I'm lucky it wasn't in my hair, she thought. "Larry, you're so clumsy sometimes."

[<u>Riley</u>: Did I just say Larry's clumsy? I did! But you don't say something like that about a boy you have a crush on, right?]

"Sorry," Larry said. He started stirring the paint, slopping some over the side of the can. When he reached for the brushes, he almost knocked the can over. "Whoa!" he cried. "I've got it!" He steadied the can, getting green paint all over the palms of his hands.

Riley rolled her eyes again. "Same old Larry," she said.

[<u>Riley</u>: Wait a sec—did I just say, "Same old Larry"? I did! And he is! Sure, his eyes are kind of nice, and he's got muscles I never noticed. But so what? He's the same old goofy Larry. No wonder I couldn't imagine kissing him! This is the crush that never was!]

Riley grabbed a brush and started painting. What a relief, she thought. She'd never had a crush on Larry. But she had been jealous of Sierra. She was getting all of Larry's attention.

But I don't want *that* kind of attention, Riley figured out. I don't want him as a boyfriend! I want him as a friend. And I've got that.

End of story, Riley thought. Except I have to make it up with Sierra. A*nd* get the garden ready!

The flowers still hadn't arrived by the time Riley and Larry had finished painting the slats, so they helped Lauren and Shane put the last of the mulch around the trees and bushes, which didn't take long. And the flowers still hadn't arrived.

"He said the truck left an hour ago!" Riley cried after calling the garden store again. "The driver hasn't called in, and there's no way to get in touch with him!"

"Maybe he got lost," Larry suggested.

"Trying to find the library?" Shane asked skeptically. "His truck probably broke down."

"Don't say that!" Riley moaned. "Besides, wouldn't he have called the store?" She glanced around. The slats were still wet, so they couldn't be varnished yet. There was nothing left to do but cross her fingers and wait for the flowers.

Half an hour went by. Shane and Lauren had to leave. Larry stayed and swept the stone pathways. Riley kept touching the painted slats and coming away with green fingertips.

More time went by. Way too much time. Riley tried the garden store, but the man still hadn't heard from the driver. Larry dug out his snack and polished off a banana and a bag of pretzels.

"Come on, Riley, eat some of this," Larry urged her, opening a bag of trail mix. "It'll give you lots of energy."

"For what?" Riley said. She couldn't stand waiting around like this!

After pacing for a minute, Riley thought of something she could do—call Sierra and apologize for the way she'd been acting. It wouldn't be easy, but it was definitely as important as the garden.

She took her cell phone to the farthest corner of the garden so Larry wouldn't overhear. Then she punched in Sierra's number.

"Don't hang up!" Riley said the second her friend answered. "I know you're mad and I totally don't blame you. But I can explain. Please?"

"Well, okay," Sierra agreed reluctantly.

"I thought I had a crush on Larry, but I don't," Riley told her. Then she quickly explained everything. "Please don't stay mad," she begged.

"You made me so angry," Sierra said. "It's like you were trying to get rid of me or something."

"I know," Riley admitted. "I felt terrible about it."

"You did?" Sierra asked. "Then why did you do it?"

Riley didn't have an answer for her. "Can we just say it was temporary insanity?" she asked. "Sierra, I'm really, really sorry!"

Sierra sighed. "Oh, Riley, it's okay," she said. "I'm just glad you figured everything out."

"Me, too!" Riley said. "Uh, Sierra, could you not tell

Larry about this? You know, it's way too embarrassing."

Sierra laughed. "I'll keep it a secret, promise."

"Thanks! Oh, wait, hang on a sec!" Riley glanced to the front of the garden. A pickup truck had just backed in. She started toward it. "I think the flowers are here!" she said into the phone.

"Really? They're kind of late, aren't they?"

"Tell me about it," Riley said. "Yes! It's the flowers! Larry and the driver are unloading them now."

Riley suddenly stopped walking. The flowers had definitely arrived. But there were hundreds of them! Flat after flat of little cardboard pots holding petunias and pansies and marigolds and …

And we have to dig a hole for every single one! Riley thought in a panic. And water them. And mulch them. And finish the benches!

"Sierra?" Riley said.

"What?"

"Helllllllp!" Riley cried.

chapter
thirteen

"**T**here she is!" Larry cried twenty minutes after Riley got off the phone. "Hi, Sierra!" He ran over and gave her a kiss.

And I don't mind, Riley thought. This is so great!

"I brought two fans and some extension cords, Riley," Sierra said, holding them. "It'll go faster that way."

"Good thinking," Riley told her. "Okay, here's the plan—the slats are finally dry, so I'll put the varnish on. You guys start planting. I'll use the fans on the varnish, and then I'll come help with the flowers."

"You're the boss!" Larry said.

And not the girlfriend, Riley thought. Thank goodness I figured things out. If I hadn't, I actually could have lost two friends!

"Be careful, Riley," Larry called as he and Sierra headed toward the flower beds. "Those varnish fumes are way strong."

Riley shook her head, smiling to herself. Larry could be a pain, but he was also a pretty good friend.

She pried open the can of varnish and began brushing it onto the slats. It was getting dark, but fortunately the library had outside lights.

While Riley slathered on the varnish, Larry and Sierra planted flowers. When Riley finished drying the slats with a fan, she gave them to Larry, who screwed them onto the benches. All three of them took time out to put the benches in place. Then they went back to planting.

"I think...wait a minute," Riley said, holding a pot of petunias and gazing around. "Yes! I'm right—these are the very last flowers!"

Larry dug the hole, then stepped aside. Riley set the plant in the hole, and Sierra scooped the dirt back around it.

"That's it!" Riley cried.

"I *thought* I heard voices back here," George Watkins said, walking into the garden. "Hi, Riley. What's happening back here?"

"What's happening is we're finished!" Riley announced proudly. "Well, we have to sweep the paths again and water the flowers, but then we are totally done! What do you think, Mr. Watkins?"

George strolled around for a moment, checking the benches, the sculptures, the flowers and bushes. Then he walked back to Riley with a big smile on his face. "I don't mind admitting when I'm wrong," he said. "I wasn't sure you could handle this, Riley, but you did. It looks spectacular!"

Yes! Riley thought. "Thanks, Mr. Watkins. We're going to finish up now and then go, okay?"

"You bet," he agreed. "You've definitely earned a rest. Thanks again, Riley. It's fantastic."

Fifteen minutes after George left, Riley and Sierra and Larry stopped working. The paths were swept clean. The sculptures and benches looked perfect. The flowers were beautiful, colorful, and ready to grow.

"It looks great!" Sierra said.

"Awesome," Larry agreed. "Like Mr. Watkins said, you did it, Riley."

"*We* did it," Riley said with a grin. Standing between them, she put her arms around their waists. "Thanks, guys!"

"Okay, Quinn, I'm ready for another balloon," Chloe said, standing on a chair in the Sunnyview lounge on Saturday afternoon.

Quinn hoisted up a red balloon. "This is the next-to-last one," she said. "The lounge is really looking great, Chloe."

"Yeah," Amanda said, passing by with an armful of paper plates and cups. "It's really nice of you to give Mr. Simms a party. I bet he'll be totally surprised."

"I hope so," Chloe said. "Are Mrs. Steiner and Mrs. Lowe coming?"

"Definitely," Quinn said. "They can't wait." She

handed Chloe the last balloon and went over to help Amanda at the food table.

Lennon came into the lounge just as Chloe taped up the last balloon. "What's up?" he asked.

"A party," Chloe said, hopping down from the stool. "It's Mr. Simms's birthday. Mrs. Scanlon and Mrs. Davidson are coming, so you might as well wait here for them."

"A party, huh?" Lennon glanced around. Amanda and Quinn were setting paper plates and cups and big bottles of soda onto a long table. "I'm guessing it's a surprise."

"You guessed right," Chloe told him. "But that's not the only surprise."

"Oh?" Lennon looked curious. "What is it?"

"You'll just have to wait and see," Chloe told him. "But I promise you—it'll be awesome."

Chloe went into the lobby just as Sierra and Alex and the rest of The Wave were coming through the front doors. Riley and Larry were with them. Chloe had called them that morning, and they'd all agreed to do her a favor and play for the party.

"Thanks for coming, you guys!" Chloe said. "Hey, how was the grand opening of the library, Riley?"

"I don't know about the library, but the garden was a major hit!" Riley grinned. "Mr. Watkins kept showing it off and telling everybody I'd made it happen."

"Well, you did," Chloe told her with a smile. Then she pointed toward the lounge. "You can set up in there. Wait—Riley! Where's Tedi?"

"She just drove up," Riley told her.

Good, Chloe thought. Everything was in place. She hurried down the hall to Mr. Simms's apartment and rang the bell. "Mr. Simms?" she called.

"Hold your horses!" The doorknob rattled loudly. Mr. Simms pulled the door open. "Chloe? I didn't know you were coming today."

"I didn't tell you I was," she said. "I wanted to surprise you."

He frowned. "I'm seventy-eight years old. I don't need any surprises."

"Wrong. You're seventy-nine," Chloe shot back. She handed him a small package wrapped in shiny red paper. "Happy birthday, Mr. Simms. Open it!"

Totally surprised, he took the gift and tore off the paper. "A camera!" he said, staring at it.

"A disposable one," Chloe told him. "I mean, I know you probably have a totally professional camera, but I wanted to get you something you could use right now without bothering with film and flashbulbs and everything."

"Well…thank you, Chloe." Mr. Simms cracked a smile. Then he frowned again. "What do you mean, 'right now'?"

Chloe grinned. "Another surprise. Actually, two more. Come on!"

They walked down the hall and through the lobby. Chloe stopped at the door to the lounge and peeked in. Good, the band was ready. Fifteen or twenty people from the retirement home were there, including the cousins.

Chloe led Mr. Simms into the lounge. "Surprise!" everyone shouted. "Happy birthday!"

"Oh, my…" Mr. Simms gazed around, practically speechless.

Chloe signaled to Amanda, who dimmed the lights. The band hit a chord, and suddenly Tedi strode through the door, looking totally hot in the slinky red dress. She was pushing a cart with the cake Manuelo had baked. A fiery sparkler stood in the center of the cake.

Smiling and gorgeous, Tedi approached Mr. Simms and sang "Happy Birthday" in a deep, sultry voice.

"Oh, my," Mr. Simms repeated, staring at Tedi.

"That's your third surprise," Chloe told him. "A pretty lady!"

Mr. Simms shook his head and laughed. "You sure know how to throw a party, Chloe!"

Tedi finished the song and held out her arms to Mr. Simms. Still laughing, he handed his cane and camera to Chloe and began dancing with Tedi.

This is so great, Chloe thought. She glanced around. Quinn was dancing with Lennon. The cousins were dancing with each other. Amanda was handing out cups of soda and Riley was rolling her eyes at something Larry was saying. Then they began to dance, too.

The party was perfect. Chloe pointed the camera at a smiling Mr. Simms and snapped a shot. In fact, it was totally spectacular.

mary-kate olsen   **ashley** olsen

so little time

Chloe
and Riley's

SCRAPBOOK

Here's a sneak peek at

BOOK 5

Starring You and Me

When we reached my car, Brian gently turned me toward him. "Ashley," he said, "there's something I have to tell you."

"What is it?" I asked. I gulped in anticipation.

Brian stared into my eyes for a moment.

Say it, I silently willed him. Say you want to get back together!

But instead of saying anything, Brian suddenly shook his head. He mumbled something and stared down at his feet.

"Brian, what's wrong?" I asked.

"Sorry, Ashley. It's just—some other time."

I stood there a moment, feeling kind of stunned. What had happened? I didn't know what to say, so I got into my car and turned on the ignition.

"Wait!" Brian said, leaning down to look at me through the window.

I gazed up at him, wondering what he could possibly have to say.

"Ashley," he declared, "you are the coolest girl I have ever met."

"Thanks, Brian." I smiled, relieved. "So, are you free tomorrow night? We could go for a walk on the beach."

It was the most romantic thing I could think of to do. Like the night at MusicFest, when we took a walk under the stars and Brian sang "Blue Eyes" to me for the first time.

"I think Penny and I are rehearsing tomorrow night."

"Okay, what about the day after?" I asked. "We could go out to dinner, see a movie."

Brian hesitated. He looked uncomfortable. "I don't know, Ashley. Can I give you a call tomorrow?"

"Ummm . . . sure," I said. I put the car in gear, waved good-bye, and pulled out of the parking lot.

As I made my way home, I thought hard about the evening and Brian's strange behavior. Maybe he was worried about the long-distance thing, too, I reasoned. I couldn't blame him.

But all the signs he had given me—every single one—told me that if things kept going the way they were, I had nothing to worry about.

I was sure Brian and I would be dating again soon. And we would manage to make it work this time—especially if he moved to Los Angeles.

WIN *A MARY-KATE AND ASHLEY*
Secret Crush Prize Pack!

TWENTY LUCKY WINNERS WILL RECEIVE:

- **A *CRUSH COURSE* videogame**
- **Cool journal and pen**
- **Stationery from the *mary-kateandashley* brand**
- **Lip gloss from the *mary-kateandashley* brand**
- **An autographed copy of**
  so little time #6 : Secret Crush

20 GRAND PRIZE WINNERS!

SO LITTLE TIME
Secret Crush Prize Pack Sweepstakes

OFFICIAL RULES:

1. No purchase necessary.

2. To enter complete the official entry form or hand print your name, address, age, and phone number along with the words "SO LITTLE TIME Secret Crush Prize Pack Sweepstakes" on a 3" x 5" card and mail to: SO LITTLE TIME Secret Crush Prize Pack Sweepstakes, c/o HarperEntertainment, Attn: Children's Marketing Department, 10 East 53rd Street, New York, NY 10022. Entries must be received no later than April 30, 2003. Enter as often as you wish, but each entry must be mailed separately. One entry per envelope. Partially completed, illegible, or mechanically reproduced entries will not be accepted. Sponsors are not responsible for lost, late, mutilated, illegible, stolen, postage due, incomplete, or misdirected entries. All entries become the property of Dualstar Entertainment Group, LLC, and will not be returned.

3. Sweepstakes open to all legal residents of the United States (excluding Colorado and Rhode Island) who are between the ages of five and fifteen on April 30, 2003, excluding employees and immediate family members of HarperCollins Publishers, Inc. ("HarperCollins"), Parachute Properties and Parachute Press, Inc., and their respective subsidiaries and affiliates, officers, directors, shareholders, employees, agents, attorneys, and other representatives (individually and collectively "Parachute"), Dualstar Entertainment Group, LLC, and its subsidiaries and affiliates, officers, directors, shareholders, employees, agents, attorneys, and other representatives (individually and collectively "Dualstar"), and their respective parent companies, affiliates, subsidiaries, advertising, promotion and fulfillment agencies, and the persons with whom each of the above are domiciled. Offer void where prohibited or restricted by law.

4. Odds of winning depend on the total number of entries received. Approximately 225,000 sweepstakes announcements published. All prizes will be awarded. Winners will be randomly drawn on or about May 15, 2003, by HarperEntertainment, whose decisions are final. Potential winners will be notified by mail and will be required to sign and return an affidavit of eligibility and release of liability within 14 days of notification. Prizes won by minors will be awarded to parent or legal guardian who must sign and return all required legal documents. By acceptance of their prize, winners consent to the use of their names, photographs, likeness, and personal information by HarperCollins, Parachute, Dualstar, and for publicity purposes without further compensation except where prohibited.

5. Twenty (20) Grand Prize Winners will win a Secret Crush Prize Pack which includes the following: a *Crush Course* videogame; a journal; pen; stationery; lip gloss; and an autographed SO LITTLE TIME: SECRET CRUSH book. Sponsor reserves the right to substitute another prize of equal or greater value in the event that the winner is unable to receive the prize for any reason. Approximate retail value per prize: $70.00.

6. Only one prize will be awarded per individual, family, or household. Prizes are non-transferable and cannot be sold or redeemed for cash. No cash substitute is available. Any federal, state, or local taxes are the responsibility of the winner. Sponsor may substitute prize of equal or greater value, if necessary, due to availability.

7. Additional terms: By participating, entrants agree a) to the official rules and decisions of the judges, which will be final in all respects; and to waive any claim to ambiguity of the official rules and b) to release, discharge, and hold harmless HarperCollins, Parachute, Dualstar, and their affiliates, subsidiaries, and advertising and promotion agencies from and against any and all liability or damages associated with acceptance, use, or misuse of any prize received in this sweepstakes.

8. Any dispute arising from this Sweepstakes will be determined according to the laws of the State of New York, without reference to its conflict of law principles, and the entrants consent to the personal jurisdiction of the State and Federal courts located in New York County and agree that such courts have exclusive jurisdiction over all such disputes.

9. To obtain the name of the winners, please send your request and a self-addressed stamped envelope (excluding residents of Vermont and Washington) to SO LITTLE TIME Secret Crush Prize Pack Sweepstakes, c/o HarperEntertainment, Attn: Children's Marketing Department, 10 East 53rd Street, New York, NY 10022 by June 1, 2003. Sweepstakes Sponsor: HarperCollins Publishers, Inc.